A TIME FOR EVERY SEASON

A TIME FOR EVERY SEASON

Shelagh Noden

ISIS

LARGE PRINT

Oxford

First published in Great Britain 2009
by
Robert Hale Limited

Published in Large Print 2010 by ISIS Publishing Ltd.,
7 Cent_____mead, Osney Mead, Oxford OX_____2 0ES
by arrangement with
Robert Hale Limited

The m_____ral _____ of the author has been _____sserted

British Library Cataloguing in Publication Data
Noden, Shelagh.
  A time for every season.
  1. Widows - - Family relationships - - Fiction.
  2. World War, 1914–1918 - - Social aspects - -
  Fiction.
  3. Farm life - - Fiction.
  4. Murder - - Investigation - - Fiction.
  5. Domestic fiction.
  6. Large type books.
  I. Title
  823.9'2–dc22

ISBN 978–0–7531–8546–9 (hb)
ISBN 978–0–7531–8547–6 (pb)

Printed and bound in Great Britain by
T. J. International Ltd., Padstow, Cornwall

CHAPTER
ONE

Meg Fraser wiped a hand over her brow, pushing back an irritating strand of dark hair that clung damply to her forehead. A little trickle of sweat ran down her back; her muscles were aching. But she wasn't going to let anyone see how exhausted she felt. There was a harvest to be got in, and with the weather threatening to break at any moment no one, least of all herself, could afford to relax.

Behind her rose the row of newly built corn stacks, golden in the sun. The rick builders were hard at work on the unfinished ricks at the end of the row, with folded seed cornbags lashed to their knees with binder twine to save wear on their corduroy trousers and protect against the vicious thistle stobs as they kneed down the sheaves to form a circle. Hard work, but immensely rewarding. Meg had once tried it herself, but her appearance in a cut-down pair of Alistair's old breeks had caused a sensation; so much so that her good friend Ellen, the doctor's wife, had felt compelled to put in a quiet word.

"You can't afford to scandalize folk like this, Meg. I know you don't give a fig what people say about you, but there's young Will to think of."

Meg frowned as she forked another sheaf up to the rick builders. She'd been forced to admit — reluctantly — that Ellen was right. After all, Braehead Farm would pass to her son Will one day, and he would need the respect of his neighbours. Having a mother who careered around in trousers would not get him that respect. Meg knew she was regarded as something of an eccentric because of the active role she'd played in the running of the farm even since before Alistair's tragic death. So, even though she knew that trousers would be far more practical, and comfortable, than the skirt she wore, she had not repeated the experiment.

Ignoring her aching back, she redoubled her efforts with the pitchfork, matching her rate of swing against the men around her. She couldn't keep up with the fittest of them, but she could outstrip the younger lads who hadn't yet learned the knack of spearing the sheaves just below the band and swinging them to the top of the rick. Young Davie McFarlane was making heavy weather of it, Meg noticed; in fact, he'd virtually stopped altogether.

"Davie, what's the matter? Do you need a break?"

Despite her anxiety to get the job finished, she put down her fork and went over to the lad. She could see he was close to tears.

"S nothin', mistress."

"Come on, Davie, I know you better than that. You've hurt your hand, haven't you? Let me see."

Davie was biting his lip to keep back the tears, but he held out his hand to Meg.

"Oh, poor lad, that looks nasty!" A large splinter — probably a thistle stob — was rammed down the boy's fingernail, and already the skin around it was looking red and inflamed.

"Right, young man, we'll get you up to the house to have this seen to." Meg glanced over to the entrance to the yard, where another of the heavily laden carts, its sides built up with hairst frames, came rumbling in for its load of sheaves to be unloaded. She recognized the driver as her neighbour, Dod Grant, and waved to him.

"I'm just going up to the house, Mr Grant. Davie needs some medical attention."

Dod, a small spare figure, his legs bowed from nearly 50 years of work as a horseman, jumped down from the cart and came over. "What's the trouble? The lad looks all right to me."

Meg held out Davie's hand for him to inspect. "He has a thistle stob down his nail —"

"He has a sore finger! The puir wee bairn!" Dod jeered at Davie, who started to protest.

"I can manage, mistress —"

"I'm sure you can, Davie, but if we don't do something about that finger now, you'll be needing Dr Jim to attend to it, and he costs money!"

She was making the only appeal she knew Dod would appreciate — notoriously tight-fisted himself, he would surely agree that it was better to avoid the doctor's fee. He came closer and seized the boy's hand himself, pressing down on the fingernail, making Davie wince with pain.

3

"Sure, that's nothing. I'll have it out with my penknife right now, then the lad can get back to his work."

He reached into his pocket but Meg stepped forward quickly. "There's no need for that, Mr Grant. I'd be grateful if you could oversee things here in the yard, and I'll take Davie up to the house."

For a moment she thought he was going to argue, but after a moment's thought he nodded. "Aye, right enough. That's women's work. You get on with that, Mistress Fraser, and I'll see to things here."

He walked away, leaving Meg seething with indignation as she escorted Davie up to the farmhouse. Dod Grant was a good neighbour, and she couldn't fault him on the way he was always ready to help out when needed. He kept his land in good order and he was a regular church attender. But she really didn't like the man. He made no secret of the fact that he thought her place was up in the house, while a hired grieve looked after the farm.

Her lips thinned. Well, people could disapprove as much as they liked, but she wasn't going to change now. And anyway, the farm was showing a tidy profit, despite the number of farm workers who had enlisted to fight the Kaiser. She was going to do her best to keep it that way so that when Will was old enough to take over there would be a thriving business for him.

As they neared the house, Ina the kitchen maid came running out.

"Oh, there you are, mistress. Mr Greig's here."

"Mr Greig? The postie?"

4

"Yes. He's sitting down, having a wee cup of tea. It's such a hot day, and he had to ride all the way up the brae on that bike of his. Poor man! He was after having a word with you."

Mildly irritated, Meg sought for an excuse. Once the postie was ensconced with a cup of tea she knew he'd be difficult to budge, and the last thing she wanted was to have to sit and make polite conversation while there was a harvest to be got in. She started to frame an excuse, but Ina's next words made her pause.

"He says he has a letter from Isobel in France."

Meg's heart skipped a beat. She had been longing to hear from her daughter, Isobel. It had been an age since her last letter, and in wartime anything could have happened. She had to resist the impulse to rush inside and grab the letter; instead she made herself stop by the back door and exchange her heavy boots for a pair of old slippers she kept there.

"Tell him I won't be a moment. I have to deal with young Davie here, he has a very nasty splinter down his nail."

"I'll do that for you, mistress," Ina offered. "I've done that sort of thing many a time."

Meg didn't hesitate long. She was sure Ina would be skilful enough with Davie, and the less time she spent up at the house the better.

"All right then. If there's any problem let me know. I'll go and talk to Mr Greig."

She went inside the solid, granite-built house, where the stone-flagged floors and dark panelled walls gave a refreshing coolness that was very welcome after the oppressive heat outside. Mr Greig was sitting in the large kitchen where a huge pot of potatoes bubbled on the range; the door and windows stood open to admit what little breeze there was.

Meg summoned up the required air of politeness. "Good morning, Mr Greig! It's a long pull up the hill on such a hot day!"

"Right enough, Mistress Fraser." The postie had courteously got to his feet as Meg came in; as she sat down he resumed his seat. "It's scorching weather; good for the harvest."

"Yes, it couldn't have been better. They say it's set to rain, though, perhaps by tonight."

Despite her calm exterior, Meg was on edge. She ran her hands over her dishevelled hair, pushing it back behind her ears. Mr Greig had brought a small bundle of letters inside, and amongst the usual business post she detected the envelope with a French stamp and her daughter's handwriting. She was desperate to get to it, but she knew that courtesy demanded she chat politely to the postman while he drank his tea and ate his scone. Only then would he condescend to give her the letters, probably with a few comments of his own. Not much escaped the sharp eyes of Andrew Greig.

Ina, having dealt with Davie, brought a freshly brewed pot of tea over and Meg gratefully accepted a cup; forking sheaves was thirsty work.

"A very welcome spot of tea, mistress," the postie commented, "and you'll be needing it yourself. You've been hard at work, I see."

6

His eyes ran over Meg's attire, an old shirt of Alistair's, its sleeves rolled up to the elbow, a threadbare skirt shortened to just below the knee. Meg sensed his mild disapproval, but ignored it.

"Yes, we have to get the job finished before the weather breaks."

She had hoped he'd take the hint and leave, but he took another leisurely sip of tea.

"I see the feed merchant's been writing to you, and the veterinary too. They'll both be wanting their payment, I don't doubt."

Despite herself, Meg had to smile. "Oh yes, you're probably right there."

"Difficult business for a woman, running a farm. A lot of responsibility. But you've made a fine job of it, mistress. A lot better than some thought you would."

"I must say I shared their doubts," Meg admitted. She knew that a lot of people had expected her to sell up after her husband's death and go back down to her native England. "But I had to do it for Will's sake."

"How is the lad?" the postman enquired.

"Well enough, thanks." Meg smiled again as she thought of her son. "Not overfond of schoolwork, but he realizes that an education is important these days even for one intending to go into farming."

"He'll be a credit to his father some day, I don't doubt. A fine man, your late husband, Mistress Fraser, very fine indeed."

"Thank you, Mr Greig." Meg's voice was slightly unsteady. She bit her lip as she glanced over at the photo of her husband, proud in his military uniform.

7

"Sometimes it's hard to think that it's over three years now, since — since Alistair was killed."

There was a respectful silence, then the postman offered, "A valiant man, Mistress Fraser, laying down his life in the service of his country. This war has a lot to answer for."

"Indeed it has." Meg spoke with feeling. "And it will have lasted four years, come September. Remember those people who said it would be over by the first Christmas?"

Andrew Greig shook his head. "If only it had. Then that daughter of yours wouldn't have got herself mixed up in it. I see she's writing to you, Mistress Fraser. I hope you'll find she's well."

"I hope so too," Meg agreed fervently, longing to get at the letter from Isobel.

"What is it she's doing over there in France? She's a nurse, is she?"

"Not exactly. She's a VAD, the lowest of the low, I'm afraid, but she loves the work, and I think she might well go into nursing when she gets back."

"An independent-minded young lady — like her mother, I don't doubt. I don't know what to make of these modern girls, Mistress Fraser, with their driving motor cars and demanding to vote, and what have you." He got to his feet reluctantly, brushing a few crumbs off his jacket. "The world isn't the place it was when I was a lad in the old queen's time."

"Indeed not," Meg agreed politely, keeping her thoughts on the matter to herself.

She escorted the postie back to his elderly bicycle and saw him off down the road, shading her eyes against the glare of the sun. Poor Mr Greig! She didn't envy him his toil around the steep winding roads of the parish, buttoned up in his heavy uniform jacket which he insisted on wearing even in the height of summer. The farm workers went about their tasks in shirtsleeves, and some of them, she knew, dispensed with their shirts entirely when out of sight of the farmhouse. Herself, she was glad of the coolness within its thick granite walls.

Leaning on the dry stone wall, she looked out over the recently harvested fields, feeling a glow of satisfaction. Another farming year almost over, a healthy balance at the bank, the workers content, the future as secure as it could be. A lot of hard work had gone into it, but she didn't begrudge a minute of it. Braehead Farm was her life now; she owed it to Alistair's memory and their son Will's future to make the business as successful as she possibly could.

There was a bank of dark cloud over in the west, and as she shaded her eyes against the sun a rumble of thunder warned Meg that she must get back to the rick yard. There was a storm on the way, rain and maybe strong wind. She should go and check that the newly built ricks were secure. She hurried round to the back door and pushed her feet into her boots, her mind troubled. The threatening storm reminded her that war still raged in Europe, and Isobel was out there. Anxiety for her daughter lanced through her, but until she was satisfied that the ricks were safe she couldn't allow herself the luxury of sitting down to read the letter.

As soon as she was sure that all was well Meg went back inside to the kitchen and picked up the sheaf of envelopes. The business ones she pushed to one side — plenty of time for them later — then she sat down at the table with Isobel's letter in her hand. Eagerly she slit it open and began to read.

A few minutes later she was staring at the closely written pages in disbelief. She could hardly comprehend what she was reading. But Isobel's neat hand spelled it out quite clearly.

I've met the most wonderful man, one of the Army doctors at the military hospital here. He's asked me to marry him, mother dear, and I've accepted. I know you'll love him when you meet him, his name is —

Meg put down the letter, and stared ahead, her eyes unfocussed. Marriage! What on earth was Isobel thinking of? Why had there been no mention of this man before? She must only just have met him. She thought back over Isobel's last letters, and yes, there had been the odd mention of a young man — several young men, in fact. No one special. And now suddenly this!

It all sounded like one of these wartime engagements, formed in the heat of the moment and so often leading to hasty marriages between people totally unsuited to one another. Marry in haste, repent at leisure. Some handsome young doctor had whispered sweet nothings to Isobel, and now she fancied herself in love.

She'd write back immediately, Meg decided, and advise caution. Wait, think things over, do nothing in haste. But then she noticed the date, and saw to her horror that the letter must have been delayed by the wartime conditions; it had been written over a month previously. Anything could have happened in that time. Isobel was over twenty-one, and so in theory needed no parental consent. And her young man, if he was a qualified doctor, he would be a few years older still. They might well be husband and wife by now.

She closed her eyes, wondering what to do. If only Alistair were here, she thought. Nothing had ever confounded him, he never lost his head. His calm certainty about life had been one of the things that had first attracted her to him, at a period in her own life when she had been desperately confused and upset. He had been such a tower of strength then, exactly what she needed now. Why, oh why, had he gone off and volunteered for the army, only to get himself killed so early on, just before the Christmas of 1914?

"I'm finished in the scullery, ma'am."

Ina's voice cut through Meg's train of thought and she looked up.

"Oh, that's good." She glanced at the tall clock that ticked steadily away in the corner. It was coming up to eleven, the traditional time for the men to stop work for the morning and rest their horses. No matter what family dramas were being played out, the old customs of the farm could not be upset.

"We'd better get the men's meal ready — they'll be in soon." She folded up the letter and put it in her pocket, deliberately repressing her feelings. There were hungry men to feed, and even in the late summer heat they liked their hot meal in the middle of the day. Here in this part of the north-east of Scotland it was customary for the farm workers to take their meals in the farmhouse kitchen rather than fending for themselves in a bothy. It meant more work for the kitchen staff, and Meg remembered with a little jolt that she had meant to do something about finding another maid to help Ina. The last girl had suddenly announced that she was leaving to become a clippie on the Aberdeen trams. Men were needed for the war effort, so women were taking their places in so many occupations.

Perhaps Ina would be next, Meg thought as she took a couple of loaves of bread out of the crock. But somehow she doubted it. Ina's young man was the third horseman at the farm, and he was known to have very old-fashioned ideas about a woman's place. No, he wouldn't countenance his intended jaunting off to work in the city. But Ina needed help, that much was obvious.

It was not until the evening, with the day's hard work behind her, that Meg could settle down in the privacy of the front parlour to finish reading Isobel's letter. It had been constantly on her mind.

She pulled it out of her pocket and reread it, trying to dampen down her anxiety. A month was a long time.

Isobel might have had second thoughts; her friends might have advised her not to be too hasty.

But in that time she might well have become Mrs — what was the man's name? She scanned through the letter, looking for the information she sought. It can't be too bad, she told herself firmly. Isobel's a sensible girl, she wouldn't do anything rash. Things could be worse.

Then as she read the last paragraph of her daughter's letter, the sheet fell from her hands and she slumped back into her chair.

No, she had been wrong. They couldn't possibly be worse.

CHAPTER
TWO

"Hold still while I put some stitches in for you. You're a lucky fellow — an inch or two higher and you'd have sliced through the artery. Then all the stitching in the world wouldn't have helped you."

Dr James Nicol squinted at the needle he was trying to thread. His eyesight wasn't what it was, he had to concede; even going over to the window didn't help. He raised his voice and called for his wife.

"Ellen! Can you help me with this?"

"Coming, dear."

His wife came so quickly into the room that Dr Jim suspected she had been waiting outside for just such a call. He smiled at her as she deftly threaded the needle and held it out to him. "Have you got hot water and iodine, dear?" she asked him.

"I have. Thank you."

He pushed his glasses further up his nose and bent to examine the gash on the man's leg. "Scythe, you say?"

"Aye, Doctor."

"Hmm, well, it's a good clean cut, it should mend well. But you'll have to keep off this leg for a while. It will stiffen up, you know."

"I can't keep off it, Doctor. I have the croft to run."

Dr Jim pursed his lips as he stitched. These crofters didn't have it easy, he reflected; all too often they worked their land single-handed, or helped only by a wife and any children who were old enough. Illness or accident was a major crisis.

"Where's your croft, did you say? Doesn't it border on Mrs Fraser's farm at Braehead?"

"It does, Doctor, right enough."

"Then why don't you ask her if she could spare a man to give you a hand for a few days? I know you've been helping her with the harvesting, so it will put you under no obligation. Merely a favour returned." Seeing the man's hesitation, he went on, "Or I could ask my wife to put in a word for you if you'd prefer."

"That would be very good of you, Doctor, if you would."

Dr Jim finished off the stitching, then bandaged up the man's leg. "Right. I'll be over to see you one of these days on my way past, and woe betide you if I catch you out in the fields. Remember what I said."

"Aye, I will that. And how much do I owe you, Doctor?"

Dr Jim named a figure that was about a third of what his colleagues in the city would have charged. He would have liked to make no charge at all, but he knew that the crofter's pride would be offended. Even so, it was not unexpected when the man said, "I'd be obliged, sir, if it could wait until the end of the month when I'll have a little money coming in? If it's no trouble —"

"It's no trouble at all."

The doctor got to his feet, wincing a little at the pain in his hip as he did so. He called again to his wife. "Ellen, is Donald about? I'd like him to run this patient home."

"He's not back from town yet, dear." His wife's tone was anxious. "Perhaps I could do it."

"No, no, you'll be busy with the cooking. I'll do it myself."

"There's no need, Doctor —"

"Nonsense! I'm not having my good stitches burst open by you gallivanting around. I'll drive you back in the trap and let your wife know what's to be done. You just sit there until I'm ready."

Later, over lunch with his wife, Dr Jim discussed the morning's events.

"I called in on Meg Fraser myself on my way back from dropping that fellow off. I asked her if she could spare a man to help out for a while, and she agreed straight away."

"Of course she did, dear. Not many people can withstand your powers of persuasion."

Dr Jim let that pass; it had become a standing joke between the pair of them. "She didn't look too well though, I thought," he went on.

"Oh dear. She works so hard though, I'm not surprised. And she's so thin. Did you prescribe some of your famous pick-me-up?"

16

"No, it wasn't that sort of unwell. She looked preoccupied — worried. I hope she hasn't had bad news about Isobel."

His wife was silent for a few moments, then she said, "I'll pop round there tomorrow. I promised her some blaeberry jam, so I'll take a couple of jars round. She might like a chat."

"Good." He sighed. "Children are a worry, aren't they, Ellen? And it doesn't lessen as they get older."

"You have no cause to worry about our daughters, dear. Both happily married and settled —"

"I'm not thinking about the girls. Is Donald not back yet?"

"No, he isn't."

"That's very inconsiderate of him, missing a meal like that. I —"

Dr Jim was interrupted by their housekeeper popping her head round the door. "Excuse me, sir, there's a man here — he says his child is having convulsions. He wants you to come."

The doctor was on his feet. "I'll be right there. Have you asked Fred to get the trap ready?"

"Yes, sir."

Ellen ran to get her husband's coat. "It's threatening rain, I'm afraid, dear. I hope you get home before it starts."

But the doctor was not so lucky. He was able to help the feverish child, and even received prompt payment for his services, but he had gone barely a mile of the return journey before the heavens opened. He was soaked to the skin within minutes, so there seemed no point in trying to find shelter and wait for the rain to stop. Grimly he pressed on.

His bad hip ached, aggravated by the jolting of the trap over the rough road. He shifted uncomfortably in his seat, trying, and failing, to get more comfortable. Ellen was right, he thought wearily, it really was time that he called it a day and retired from his work. But who would take over a small country practice like this? There was more money to be made far more easily elsewhere.

At one point he had hoped that his son would take over from him. A sufferer from asthma, Donald had been exempt from military service and had gone so far as to enrol at medical school in Aberdeen, but after less than a year he had opted out, saying that medicine was not for him. He seemed to have no clear idea of what career he wanted to follow and Dr Jim shook his head sadly as he thought of his son. An occupation of some sort was a necessity for him, the practice didn't make enough money to support him in a life of idleness, even if Dr Jim had been prepared to countenance it, which he wasn't. Donald's asthma was sufficiently well under control for him to hold down a job, and it was time he set about finding one.

Dr Jim remembered the privations he'd had to go through as a student. It hadn't been easy, and when he'd qualified it had been tempting to take a well-paid city practice. But he had been drawn back to his roots in the country, where he felt his skills were needed. And it had been a good life, on the whole. He hoped he would be able to find someone who shared his views. Until then he'd just have to keep soldiering on.

He was relieved when he arrived home, and with difficulty climbed down from the trap. Fred came up to attend to the horse and Ellen ran out of the house, her expression deeply concerned.

"Jim, you're soaked through! I knew you would be. Mrs Michie has got some water heated — you must get in a hot bath straight away."

"I'm fine —"

"Rubbish! You'll be in bed with double pneumonia if you're not careful, and then what will happen to your patients? You're not doing them any favours by trying to be brave. And your hip looks to be stiffening up — oh, what are we going to do with you?"

She fussed around him like a mother hen, and after a small initial resistance Dr Jim gave in and let himself be looked after. It was a pleasant feeling.

But as he took off his wet things and prepared to soak in a hot bath, he couldn't help wondering how long he could go on.

A couple of miles down the road, in a dilapidated croft house, Jeannie Duncan faced her mother across the kitchen table. Around her, lines of washing in various stages of dryness hung steamily. The fire burned brightly, its heat adding to the close, oppressive atmosphere.

"Ma, do I have to go?"

Her mother, tight-lipped, bent over her ironing, not looking up at her daughter. "Yes, you do."

"Can't I stay here and help you? I'm a good help, really I am. I hung all this up —"

"Wee Lizzie can help me with that. No, it's a good position I've got you, and it was just by chance I bumped into Mistress Fraser at the post office this morning and she happened to say she was looking for a girl —"

"Mistress Fraser! Everyone's scared of her! They say she dresses like one of the men."

"What does that matter? She'll pay you well."

"But Ma!" Jeannie stared around desperately. "You know how much I want to stay on at the school. Miss Henderson said I was her best scholar — she said I could try for the Academy. In time I could train as a teacher at one of the big schools in the city. I can't leave now. Please."

At that her mother slammed down the iron and stared back at her daughter, stony-eyed. "I've made up my mind, Jeannie, and that's that. We can't have a great girl like you eating her head off and not bringing anything in. I'm on my own, don't forget, and I have the six of you to think about. I have to slave in here all day and every day taking in other folks' washing and even so it hardly makes ends meet."

"Perhaps I could work for Mrs Fraser in the evenings and weekends —"

"Don't be daft. She wants a live-in maid, and that's what you're going to be. So you'll have to leave the school. I'll send word to Miss Henderson on Monday."

"But Sandy's staying on at the school. You're not making him leave!"

"That's different. He's a boy."

Stung into silence at the injustice of it, Jeannie turned on her heel and flung out of the room. Hot angry tears welled up in her eyes but she blinked them back, not wanting to show any sign of weakness. She slammed the door on the hot steamy kitchen and went outside into the yard. The rain had dwindled to a fine drizzle — too much for the wet clothes to be hung out to dry but not enough to prevent her running up the hill to her favourite place among the rocks. She ran quickly through the bracken, heedless of the wet droplets that clung to her, and panting flung herself down in the shelter of the largest boulder.

Then at last, knowing she was unobserved, she let the tears come. It wasn't fair, it just wasn't fair! Why could her mother not understand?

Her father would have understood, she was sure. But he had gone off to the war and never come back, like Mr Fraser at Braehead, and so many others.

She looked down the hill at their cottage, small and unkempt. The yard was weedy and the outbuildings decaying. Sandy did his best, she knew, but he didn't have enough time or experience to look after the place properly. Perhaps, she thought, with a last surge of optimism, she could offer to stay at home and work her fingers to the bone trying to look after the tiny croft and make some sort of profit out of it. Then she could study in the evenings — surely Miss Henderson would help her? Anything rather than be sent away. Once she was a maid at Braehead, that would be the end of everything.

A thought came to her, and she raised her head and shouted defiantly, "I won't go to Braehead; I'll run away first!"

"Don't be such a daftie."

There was a rustling above her and then someone jumped down from the boulder above her. Jeannie tensed, then, when she saw who it was, she relaxed. "Oh, it's you."

"Aye." Her twin brother Sandy sat down beside her companionably and put an arm round her shoulders. Jeannie said nothing, ashamed that her outburst had been overheard.

At last she ventured, "Has she told you, then?"

"She has. I was milking the goat, and when I heard you slamming out of the house like that I thought the place had taken fire at least. But it's only about having to leave the school."

"*Only!*"

"Ach, don't make such a fuss!" Sandy roughly patted his sister's arm. "Don't you know everything they can teach you there already? You're always the top of the class. Myself, I'd be out of the door tomorrow if Ma'd let me."

Jeannie wiped her eyes. "It's all wrong, Sandy. You should have been the girl and I the boy." Ignoring his indignant protest she went on, "Then Ma would've let me stay on at school and you could leave."

"To be a maid at Braehead? No thanks!"

22

She laughed. "I can't imagine you in a cap and apron. What a sight!" Then she became more serious. "But I wonder if you could be the one to leave and get a job? You'd like that, wouldn't you?"

"I'd like it fine. I want to be a horseman, Jeannie, like our father. I'd start at the bottom, as the orra loon, and work my way up."

"Well, why don't we say that to Ma? Then you'd have the wage coming in, and I could stay on at school, and go to high school and everything. Everyone would be happy that way."

Sandy shook his head. "It wouldn't work. Because Ma doesn't want me to do farm work, she wants me to have an office job. You know that."

"You'd hate that."

"You bet I would."

"So can't we make her see she's making us both miserable? If we did it our way, I'd be a teacher and you'd make your way to be first horseman on a big farm, or maybe a grieve, or even own a farm yourself. You could do that, Sandy." Jeannie's eyes were shining. "Let's go and talk to her. If we both do it, she'll realize. She must."

Sandy didn't share her optimism. "I doubt she will. But don't say anything until the washing's dry. Then she'll be in a better mood."

"Good idea," Jeannie jumped to her feet. "I'll go and help her with it, and I'll collect the eggs, and I'll make supper, and —"

"You won't have time for anything else."

Jeannie's jaw was set. "I'll make time."

But Sandy was right; the plan didn't work, even though they didn't broach the subject until the day's washing was all dried and ironed, the evening meal eaten and the washing up done, and their mother was sitting by the fire with a cup of tea. She was still adamant.

"No, Jeannie, it's not right that Sandy should be denied his chance. And it's a good situation up at Braehead. You'll find Mistress Fraser very kind, much better than many a one you could be working for."

"But Sandy doesn't want this chance!" Jeannie pleaded. "He'll hate working in an office. He wants to work with horses like Father did —"

Her mother flared up. "Don't you argue with me, my girl! It's all arranged, and I'm not changing my mind."

"But Ma —" Sandy began, but she turned on him.

"So your father was good with horses, was he? And where did that get him? Look around you!"

There was silence. Jeannie looked around the small room — at the old-fashioned grate that smoked on windy days, the bare cement floor with only a faded rag rug in front of the fire, the shabbily curtained box bed in the corner where her mother slept with the youngest child, the poor sticks of furniture. Her heart sank.

"No, I want something better for you, son," Mrs Duncan went on vehemently. "I want you to make your way in the world, to have a proper job where you'll be respected. Not this!"

There was silence, broken only by the drumming of rain on the tin roof. There was no more to be said.

Later that night in the tiny attic room she shared with her sisters, Jeannie lay awake. So she'd have to go to Braehead, there was no way out of it. She'd considered running away but common sense held her back. That would be a foolish thing to do, and wouldn't help her ambitions at all.

But perhaps Mrs Fraser wasn't as scary as she appeared. Maybe she would let her study in the evenings or something, as long as it didn't interfere with her work. She'd take her few books with her, she decided, and keep them in her room. Because she was simply not going to give up on her education, no matter what it cost her.

Dod Grant sat opposite Meg in the parlour, a cup of tea precariously balanced on his knee. He looked out of place in the neat surroundings. It was well known that he had started life as a farm boy and had worked his way up through the ranks of horsemen before he had managed to buy his own farm, with no time to acquire any social graces. Meg had nothing against him for that. In fact, she admired his tenacity, which matched her own. Nevertheless she wished silently that he would hurry up and get to the point of his visit. Surely it couldn't be simply a social call? Dod would not want to waste time on such frivolities. She hoped she'd be able to concentrate when he eventually got to the point — since that letter from Isobel her mind had been in a whirl. She'd had several attempts at writing a reply, but torn them all up. Finding the right tone was difficult — not too preachy, but leaving Isobel in no doubt about what she felt. She'd try again that evening once Dod had gone, she promised herself.

Meanwhile she had to make conversation; the long silences were beginning to be hard to take.

"That storm we had was quite a relief, don't you think, Mr Grant? The heat was getting very oppressive."

"Aye. The fields needed a drop of rain."

"So they did."

Silence. Meg tried again. "Have you had any problems with staff deserting you? My last maid went off to work as a clippie."

Dod shook his head. "Old Annie McKenzie has been with me for years, she won't be going anywhere. She's all the help I need in the house. I'm a man of simple tastes."

"No harm in that, Mr Grant," Meg congratulated herself at getting such a long speech out of the man. "Last time I was in your house I remember it was very well kept."

"Aye, over a year since, wasn't it? Ye must come again."

Meg blinked. An invitation to visit from Dod Grant was something of a rarity. Had he suddenly decided to develop a social life? While she was wondering how to reply, he spoke again.

"I'd like it fine if ye'd come over and see the place some time. Take a look round the buildings, see the beasts."

"Why, thank you, Mr Grant, that's very —"

"Because I've been thinking, Mistress Fraser." Unexpectedly, Dod put his cup and saucer down and

26

leaned forward. His whole frame seemed alight with enthusiasm; his sparse moustache bristled. "I'm minded that our two farms — Overton and Braehead — would go very well together. As it stands they do well enough, don't get me wrong, but as one unit they could do even better."

Meg stared at him. She was completely at a loss. "It would make a very big farm," she said at last.

Dod didn't seem to notice her hesitation. "Indeed it would and all the better for it. Think of the future, Mistress Fraser. Mechanization. Tractors. Horses are a thing of the past; farms will be larger in future. Just think of what we could do with all that land. We could have more beasts, we could grow more grain."

Meg looked at him. His usually expressionless features were alight with enthusiasm. Why, he really wants to do this, she thought.

"Are you offering to sell?" she asked slowly.

"Ach, no. I'm minded that we could combine the two. Ye must see what I'm getting at."

Some sort of partnership, Meg thought without enthusiasm. But she felt she had at least to consider the prospect seriously. There was something to be said for it, and there was her son Will's future to think of. Dod had never married, and perhaps in time Will might inherit the two farms.

Dod was looking at her intently. She began to feel slightly embarrassed. "Ye'll consider it then?" he urged. "I don't want to rush ye, mind, but I'm hoping ye'll give my offer some thought?"

"Well, I'll certainly do that," she said, wanting to be free of him and have time to think. "Perhaps you could get me some details to look over."

"I'll do that, mistress." He got to his feet and picked up the flat cap he always wore, twirling it between his fingers. "Good evening to ye."

"Good evening."

Meg went to the door with him as politeness demanded. He had come on foot — "no point in harnessing one of the horses when it's only a step" — and she stared after him as he trudged off down the brae, recalling how he had talked about "we" could do this, "we" could do that. She wasn't sure that she wanted to be in such a close business relationship with Dod. She would have to think over his offer very carefully.

She shut the door and leaned against it for a moment, eyes closed. First Isobel, now this. Why was life so complicated?

But now she had to write that letter.

CHAPTER
THREE

Meg stopped by the postbox and stared down at the envelope in her hand. Should she post it, or take the letter home for yet another revision? Did it really say everything she wanted to say to her daughter? Did it strike the right tone, or would Isobel be offended by what she saw as unwarranted interference?

She sighed. The fireplace was already full of screwed-up balls of paper, the discarded earlier attempts at her letter to Isobel. It was high time the thing was sent. So without giving herself time for any more hesitation, she reached out and dropped the letter in the box.

There. It was done.

She walked quickly away from the postbox, picturing Isobel's reaction when she read the letter. It would hurt the girl to learn that her mother was not overjoyed about her impending marriage, that she counselled delay and expressed doubt about the whole thing.

Meg bit her lip. She didn't want to upset Isobel, especially when she was already suffering hardship, maybe even risking her life, out in war-torn France. But she knew in her bones that this marriage — should it happen — would be a disaster. The odds were stacked too heavily against it.

"Look out!" The warning shout brought Meg swiftly back to reality. She stepped back with a gasp, realizing that she had almost walked in front of the doctor's pony and trap. Ellen Nicol was driving; she leaned down in concern.

"Are you all right, Meg? That was rather too close for my liking."

"I'm fine, Ellen." Meg managed a shaky smile. "I'm so sorry. I can't imagine what I was doing. What a good job old Solomon is so placid."

Ellen reached out and patted the pony. "It would take something like an earthquake to unsettle him. But I'm glad I've met you — I was just on my way up to Braehead with some jam. If you've finished your business I can give you a ride up."

"Thank you." Meg accepted gratefully and scrambled up into the trap beside Ellen. The incident had quite shaken her and she was glad of the lift.

"You're looking tired, Meg," Ellen commented as the pony trotted unconcernedly along. "Now that the harvest's safely in, you should take things easy."

Meg gave her friend a wry glance. "If only I could! But we have to start on the winter ploughing while the weather holds and there's the repairs to be done to the barn —"

"There's always something! Can't you let someone else shoulder the burden for once?"

"Don't you start!" Meg retorted, smiling. "People are always telling me I should get a grieve and let him do the work, but honestly, Ellen, what would I do then? I've been running the farm ever since Alistair was killed. I'd be lost without it. I'm not the sort to sit in an armchair and do fine sewing, or entertain the minister to cups of tea. Can you see me a lady of leisure? Now can you?"

"All right, you win! But don't work yourself too hard."

"I won't do any more than what's necessary. I want the farm to be in a good state for when Will takes over."

"I'm sure it will be. He's a lucky lad to have a mother who works so hard for him."

"I owe it to Alistair," Meg said quietly. "The least I can do in his memory is ensure that his only son has a respected place in the community."

There was silence for a moment as Ellen halted the trap outside the farmhouse, then she pressed her friend's hand. "He'll have that, believe me. He's the image of his father, a grand lad. You can be proud of him, Meg." Then she added, "And what about that daughter of yours? How is she getting on? The postie tells me you had a letter from her the other day."

Meg laughed. "Nothing's secret round here! Yes, we did have a letter. Come in and have a cup of tea and I'll bring you up to date."

Later, over tea and scones with blaeberry jam, Meg at last found courage to share what was troubling her.

"Isobel's fine, but she did have some news that shook me rather. She told me she's planning to get married.

To a doctor called David who works in the same field hospital."

"Oh!" Ellen paused. She'd been going to say "How wonderful!" but something in Meg's expression stopped her. "How do you feel about it?" she asked cautiously.

"Oh, Ellen!" Meg bit down on her lower lip, and the older woman could see she was close to tears. "It's a ghastly situation — of all the people she could have chosen!"

"I don't understand."

Meg hesitated. She couldn't tell Ellen the real story. Not just yet, anyway. She'd have to tell her only part of the truth for now.

"He's from Kent — my part of the world. Same town actually. That's how they came to be introduced. But the trouble is that long ago there were difficulties between the two families," she said at last. "Very serious difficulties —"

"And do David and Isobel know about this?"

"No, they don't."

"I see," Ellen was silent for a while, then she said, "But couldn't a marriage between the two of them bring about a healing process? It might be just what's needed."

"No!" Meg spoke more forcefully than she'd intended, and Ellen looked at her in surprise. "No," she repeated. "I think it would be a disaster."

Will Fraser stared at his algebra homework. If only he could wave a magic wand and have it all done in the twinkling of an eye. He so much wanted to go out to the barn and see the new collie pups that were born two days ago. But he knew his mother wouldn't let him out of the house until he'd got the wretched homework done.

She wouldn't understand how he felt about it. Figures were no problem to her; he'd seen her totting up the farm accounts in her head, just like that. He must take after his father, he decided. Pa was never good at that sort of thing, he was content to leave it all to his wife.

Will frowned, remembering his father. He knew that some people said that Meg Fraser was the one who ran Braehead Farm, not her husband. One of the boys at school had taunted Will with it, sneering that Will's father was not the master in his own home. Will had left him with a bloody nose on account of it, and his mother had been very angry when she'd heard. But his father had seemed resigned, even proud.

"She's a fine woman, your mother," he'd said. "Clever, too, and a lot of people can't forgive her for that. They think a woman's place is the kitchen, not the farm office. But I don't hold with that, and I hope you don't either."

A week after that his father had set sail for France and Will had never seen him again. And after a time of intense grief his mother had carried on running the farm, and Will had carried on at school. Everyone said it was what his father would have wanted. It was only a matter of time, he thought, then he'd be able to leave and work on the farm. That is, if his mother would let him. He scratched his head worriedly. Suppose she wanted to carry on being in charge? Will wasn't sure how he would cope with that. With a sigh he turned back to the blank page of his exercise book and resumed the struggle with quadratic equations.

"That's not the answer." A voice came from behind him, and Will turned sharply. At first he thought it was his mother speaking, then he saw it was the new maid. She was looking over his shoulder at the book.

Annoyance flared in him. "What do you know about it, Jeannie Duncan?"

"More than you'd think. You've got it all wrong. Shall I show you?"

"Go on then," he challenged, expecting to call her bluff. But to his surprise she sat down, took up a pencil and quickly worked out the equation. It looked convincing too.

"There you are."

"How do I know you've got it right?"

"You'll just have to trust me, if you can't work it out yourself."

"What about the rest?"

"No problem."

Her pencil flew over the paper with Will watching in awed amazement. "Thanks," he said when at last she stood up. "Where did you learn to do that?"

"At school in the village."

"But I only learned that at high school."

"Miss Henderson gave me special lessons."

"Oh. So why are you working here instead of —"

34

She jolted to her feet. "I'm sorry, I have to get on." She almost pushed past him in her hurry to get out of the room. Will wasn't sure but he thought he saw a tear glistening on the end of her lashes. He shook his head, puzzled.

But the homework was done, that was the good thing. Maybe the answers were all wrong — part of him couldn't believe that a kitchen maid could manage algebra homework — but at least he had something down on the page which hopefully would satisfy the maths master. Whistling to himself, he went out to see the puppies.

"Well done, Will," Meg said later as they sat down to supper together.

Will looked up surprised. "What for?"

"Your maths homework. I saw it lying on the table and checked it through. It's all correct."

"Oh — oh, good." Will hoped he wasn't going red; a feeling of intense guilt filled him. He didn't like to sit there and accept his mother's praise when he hadn't done the homework himself. He opened his mouth to say something, then closed it again. He couldn't get Jeannie into trouble.

"Have you seen the collie pups?" he asked, wanting to change the subject.

"Yes, I have. Adorable, aren't they? Good working dogs too, if they're anything like their parents. We should get a good price for them."

"Oh." Disappointment plummeted through Will. Once again his mother was looking at the commercial

35

side of things, like the good businesswoman she was. "Could we not keep one?" he pleaded.

His mother thought for a moment. "Well, all right, I tell you what we'll do. You keep on getting good marks for your maths, and when the puppies are old enough to go you can choose one for your own. But if the marks go down again —"

Will tightened his lips. It looked as though there was only one thing for it. He'd have to get Jeannie Duncan to keep on helping him. He so desperately wanted a dog of his own, and it looked like this was the only way.

"Thanks, Mum. I'll do my best. I'll just go and have a look at them." He pushed his chair back and got up from the table, angry with himself for planning to deceive his mother but resigned to the fact that this was the only course he could take.

He went into the kitchen, intending to have a quick word with Jeannie and tell her how the land lay. He hoped she'd agree to help him. If she was that keen on schooling, maybe it would be a pleasure for her. But she might not want to be party to deceiving his mother; he had to admit he felt bad about it himself.

Just as he got to the kitchen door there was a crash, followed by the sound of raised voices. Will hurried in to find Jeannie staring dismally at a pile of smashed crockery. The other maid, Ina, was roundly telling her off.

"What happened?" Will wanted to know.

"This clumsy lass dropped a pile of china plates! The mistress will have a fit when she finds out!"

36

"We'd better clear it up quick. I'll help you." Will, feeling that helping Jeannie was the least he could do, bent to pick up the pieces, but a shocked exclamation from the doorway made him realize he was too late.

"What ever has been going on here?"

His mother swept into the room, gazing with dismay at the shattered plates.

"I'm sorry, ma'am," Jeannie said in a small voice. "I dropped them, I don't know what happened —"

Suddenly Will spoke up. "It was my fault." He saw Jeannie staring at him in amazement, while Ina's mouth was an O of disbelief. "I came into the kitchen and bumped into her. That's what made her drop the plates."

His mother gave him an assessing glance and he did his best to meet it. After a long time she said, "Very well. In that case the money to replace them will come out of your allowance, Will. Perhaps you could be good enough to clear up the mess."

She turned and went out, leaving a silent group in the kitchen. At last Jeannie found her voice. "You shouldn't have said that. It wasn't true."

"Just as well he did though," Ina put in. "It would have made a big hole in your wages, having to pay for all that."

Will bent to pick up the larger pieces. Jeannie knelt beside him with a dustpan and brush. "Why'd you do it?"

"Because you did that homework for me. It's my way of saying thanks."

"Just for that?"

"It means a lot, I'll explain sometime. I hope you might help me with it again."

Jeannie put down her brush. "I can't. I shouldn't have done it in the first place. It's cheating."

"I know." Will hung his head. "But —"

"I tell you what. I'll show you how to do it yourself. That would make it right."

Will felt doubtful. "Yes, but I don't know if I could."

"You're just like my brother. Don't worry. I want to be a teacher, so it's good practice. We'll start tomorrow if you like."

The next morning Will got up bright and early to look at the puppies. He was just coming back to the house when he met Ina out in the yard.

She greeted him with a scowl. "That idle lassie's done it this time. You won't be able to get her out of it today."

"Why? What's happened?" Will glanced through the kitchen door, expecting to see another pile of broken dishes.

"She's still in her bed, that's what. The lazy hussy! She should be up helping me get the brose ready for the men."

"Perhaps she's ill."

"Ill!" Ina snorted. "Asleep, that's what."

Will, alarmed, hurried into the house. He could hear his mother upstairs. It could only be a matter of time before she discovered that Jeannie had overslept. With a swift look over his shoulder to check that he was unobserved, he went over to the narrow staircase that led to the maids' attic rooms above the kitchen.

"Jeannie!" he hissed.

No response.

"Jeannie!"

There was nothing for it, he would have to go and wake her himself. He knew he would be in terrible trouble if he was found out — the maids' rooms were strictly forbidden territory — but before he could think better of it he stole up the stairs.

One door was shut, the other open. He tapped on the closed door. "Jeannie!"

A muffled voice answered and he pushed open the door to the tiny bare room. Jeannie half sat up, rubbing her eyes and stifling a scream when she saw him in the doorway. He put a finger to his lips.

"You've overslept, I came to wake you. Are you unwell?"

Then he stopped as he saw the books. A pile of them beside the bed, one open on the top. A candle in a tin holder had completely burnt down.

"What on earth have you been doing? Reading?"

"Studying. I have to. I do it at night; it's my only chance."

Will was going to remonstrate with her but he stopped himself. This was neither the time nor the place.

"We'll talk about this later. Now, for heaven's sake get yourself up before my mother finds out."

He turned and tiptoed down the stairs, hoping that he could keep his mother out of the kitchen long enough to give Jeannie time to get herself up and dressed. He reached the foot of the stairs then froze. Ina had just come in through the kitchen door. Her expression changed from amazement to a cunning grin.

"Well, well. I wonder what the mistress will say when she hears where you've been?"

"Add some cascara to the list, Ellen." Dr Jim Nicol, spectacles on the end of his nose, checked the next shelf of his dispensary. "I'm sure I'm all right for calamine. I know I have some somewhere —"

"Next shelf up, dear," his wife prompted.

"Oh yes, there it is. Right next to the cooling powders. Only the top shelf left to check now."

"And you're not going to check it. I don't want you climbing up ladders with that hip of yours. Perhaps Donald will do it for you. I heard him come in a moment ago."

"Good. It will make a change for that lad to do something useful," Dr Jim said tartly.

"Don't be hard on him, dear. He's had a rough time lately. A woman gave him a white feather the other day, for not being in uniform. She wasn't to know he suffers from asthma."

"Fair enough, but it shouldn't prevent him from getting a proper job. Then he wouldn't be wandering the streets in the middle of the day. If only he'd carried on at medical school."

Ellen took her husband by the arm and led him into the kitchen. "We've gone through all this before, dear. I'm sure he'll find something eventually. Now let's have something to eat — there's a pot of broth on the range. Mrs Michie left it ready."

Her husband started to speak but before he could say anything the door opened and a tall young man came in. "Donald!" Ellen smiled at him. He was so like his father at that age, sandy-haired and rake thin. "Come and eat with us, then I'd be grateful if you could help us in the dispensary."

"Glad to. Then I was hoping to go into town."

"Again!" his father snorted. "You're never away from the place."

"Well, I've a reason for going. I wanted to talk to you about it."

Donald sat down at the table next to his father as his mother ladled out plates of broth. She could see that her son had an air of suppressed excitement, as if he had some very important news to impart. She had a sudden feeling of foreboding, remembering Meg's news about Isobel. Surely Donald couldn't be about to announce he was getting married?

Trying to maintain a calm exterior, she sat down.

"Well, spit it out, son," Dr Jim prompted. "Have you got yourself a job?"

"Not exactly." His father sighed, but Donald didn't seem to notice. "More of an opportunity."

"Go on."

"Well, a chap I know is intending to start up a garage in Aberdeen. He's asked me to go in with him."

"A garage?" Ellen queried.

"Yes. Repairing motor cars, selling petroleum, perhaps even selling cars if we get that far."

Ellen cast a glance to her husband, but he was stolidly applying himself to his soup. "Does your friend have premises?" she asked Donald.

"He has the offer of them."

"Ah."

"He needs cash," Donald explained. "As well as leasing the building, he would have to get tools and equipment. That's expensive."

"So you're saying you want some money?" his father put in.

"Well, not exactly. There's that money Aunt Julia left me —"

"But that's in trust until your twenty-first birthday."

"I know. I hoped you might see your way to a loan. I'd pay you back either next year when I'm twenty-one or when we made enough profit if that was earlier."

Dr Jim choked on his soup. While he spluttered, Ellen put a few questions to Donald. "Are you sure this is a good investment? Does your friend have any experience?"

"He worked as a mechanic in the army, then he was invalided out after he got gassed. It left him with weak lungs. But he has plenty of experience with motor vehicles."

"That's good, but what about business experience?"

"He knows a chap who would take care of that side of things."

"Hmm. So where do you come in? Except as a source of cash?"

"Well, I've always been interested in machines. I expect I could learn quickly. And you must admit that motor vehicles are the future."

"What do you think, dear?" Ellen asked her husband.

"I wouldn't touch it with a barge pole." Dr Jim was typically forthright. "That legacy from your aunt was intended to secure your future, not vanish into the pockets of some fly-by-night garage operators —"

"Dad! These are my friends you're talking about!"

"I don't care. I still think you'd be a fool to trust your legacy to some project you don't know anything about. At least get it checked out first."

"Your father's talking sense, Donald —" Ellen began, but her son had shot to his feet.

"I'm not staying here to listen to this! I might have known you'd take this attitude! First you criticize me for not having a job, then when I find an opportunity you won't back me up!"

Before Ellen could say anything else he had stormed out, banging the door behind him. Ellen and Jim looked at one another.

"I know, I know," Jim said. "You're going to tell me I handled it all wrong, and I should have been more tactful."

"Just a little, dear."

"But you must admit that I was right? We can't let him waste his money on some crazy scheme."

"We don't know that it's crazy. It might be very sensible. He seemed very enthusiastic."

"He was enthusiastic about medical school and how long did that last? A few months?"

Ellen said nothing, but inwardly she was very troubled. She didn't like to see her husband and son at loggerheads like this, but she really didn't know what to do for the best. Was Jim right to be suspicious? Or should they let Donald take the chance with his legacy?

Meg was taken aback when Dod Grant called round with his pony and trap to collect her for her visit to his farm. She had expected to walk — it was a fine September day, and the distance was only a couple of miles — but just as she was getting ready to set off Dod had turned up to collect her.

He had made an effort with his appearance too. Usually he dressed much the same as one of his farm workers, in corduroy trousers tied at the knee and an old waistcoat over his flannel shirt, but today he was resplendent in leather gaiters and a tweed jacket that smelt strongly of mothballs. Clearly he was very serious about going into partnership.

"This is very kind of you, Mr Grant," she said as they bowled along the lane, "but you shouldn't have taken the trouble."

"No trouble, Mistress Fraser. And I wanted to point one or two wee things out to ye along the way. Like those lower fields, for instance. See how we've drained them with new ditches. They'll be fit to plough this winter and I think we might get a good crop off them."

"That's very impressive." Meg was sincere in her praise. Dod's men seemed to have done a good job on the fields. They had cleared the land of stones, which they had piled up in a big cairn in a corner of the field. Further on was a field of black cattle, looking in prime condition, and then the farm itself came into view.

44

Overton farmhouse was a low, old-fashioned building, drab and strangely unkempt looking with its corrugated iron roof. Clearly the residence of a man who did not spare much thought for his own comfort. Dod must have noticed Meg's expression, for he said abruptly, "I've had an estimate to get it slated. Terrible expensive, and the tin roof keeps out the wet perfectly well, but I'm minded I'll have it done."

"It would improve the look of the house," Meg said, "and I'm sure you'd find it worthwhile in the long run. It would last a lot longer than the tin roof."

"Aye, right enough."

They stopped in the yard, and Dod handed Meg down. "I thought we might have a wee bite to eat before we look around. Would that suit ye, mistress?"

"Er — well, thank you, Mr Grant." Meg was rather reluctant, but she felt it would be impolite not to agree. She followed Dod into the house, trying not to appear too curious.

The place was scrupulously clean but spartan in its furnishings. Meg sensed that what little time Dod was inside the house he spent in the kitchen, but he insisted on showing her into a cramped front parlour, which felt damp with lack of use. Some farming papers had been pushed almost out of sight under a small table, but otherwise there was no sign of occupation.

Annie McKenzie, Dod's housekeeper, came through with a pot of tea and a plate of oatcakes. She gave Meg a glance which bore more than a trace of hostility. "I hope you find this to your liking, mistress."

"Thank you," Meg said politely. "It looks very good."

45

She remembered the rumours of Annie watering the men's broth and wondered if they were true. The tea was weak enough, and the oatcakes were leathery. She felt a stab of sympathy for Dod, having to endure this standard of cooking, but he ate and drank as if he didn't notice anything wrong. Presumably he was used to it.

At last, the uncomfortable meal concluded, the tour of the farm began. The noise of machinery greeted them in the yard, and Dod led Meg to the barn where a threshing machine was in full swing.

"Bought this last year," he announced over the racket. "We thresh twice a week."

"It's petrol driven!" Meg was impressed. At Braehead they still relied on an old steam engine, and although she had often considered investing in a petrol-driven threshing machine, she had never as yet taken the plunge to invest in the new technology. She felt slightly ashamed of herself for letting herself be overtaken by Dod Grant.

"Aye, it's the way forward." Dod seemed pleased at her approval. "Next year I'm thinking I'll buy a tractor."

He would too, Meg thought to herself, as she watched the men working. Perhaps, she thought, he would make a good partner after all. Mechanical knowledge had never been her strong point.

Up on top of the mill two of the men fed the stalks of grain into the machine while another two collected the sacks of milled corn from below. A boy collected the chaff, while another man looked after the engine. They worked efficiently enough, but Meg noticed that there was little of the friendly banter that she was used to hearing at Braehead. These men worked in virtual silence, hardly making any sign that they noticed the presence of a visitor. She was reminded of Dod's reputation as a hard master.

It was a relief to get out at last from the dusty atmosphere inside the barn into the open air, and she followed Dod around the granite buildings, stable, byre and sheds, listening carefully to his running commentary. He certainly knew his stuff, and she found herself filled with a growing sense that this was indeed the best way forward. Yes, the two farms combined would make a big property, but with more mechanization they could be as easily run together as separately. There would have to be a watertight agreement drawn up, though, and she made up her mind to see old Mr Wishart, her solicitor, as soon as she possibly could.

At length they stood together outside the front door of the farmhouse, and Meg prepared to take her leave.

"Thank you, Mr Grant, it's been a very interesting afternoon."

"Ye liked the place then? Ye liked my idea to combine the two?"

Meg did, very much so, but she didn't want to be too enthusiastic, not just yet. "I think your idea is a good one, Mr Grant, but I'd like time to think about it before I come to a decision."

"Ah. How much time would that be? I'll be honest wi' ye, Mistress Fraser, I'd hoped to see the two of us settled by New Year."

An odd turn of phrase, Meg thought, but she let it pass. "I think we might manage that," she said with a smile. "But these things are too important to be rushed, I'm sure you'll agree?"

Her answer seemed to please him. "Aye, right enough, mistress, right enough. Too important to be rushed. Well, I'll just be getting the trap to run ye back home —"

"Oh, no need for that, Mr Grant. I'm happy to walk, it's such a fine evening."

At first she thought he was going to insist, but then, plainly, the relief of not having to get out the trap again came to him and he assented.

"A good walk never did anyone any harm surely. Well, I'll be bidding ye good evening, mistress, and I hope to hear from ye bye and bye."

"You will." Meg put out her hand politely, but she was unprepared for the warmth with which her fingers were pressed between Dod's horny palms. For a crazy moment she thought he was actually going to raise her hand to his lips in some ridiculous attempt at a chivalrous gesture, but mercifully he let go and she stepped back.

"Good evening, Mr Grant." Almost without waiting for a reply, she turned and set off down the track, back towards Braehead. Once she turned and looked back, and he was still there, staring after her.

Good heavens, she thought, he can hardly wait to get the two farms joined. I'll have to make sure the agreement doesn't allow him too much say in what goes on at Braehead. It's not a takeover; simply a business partnership.

And then suddenly the awful thought struck her. Was it simply a business partnership that Dod had in mind?

CHAPTER
FOUR

"Look at them, Ma! Aren't they coming on just fine!" Will watched the puppies, enthralled. "See the one with the white nose, I reckon he's the most advanced for his age. Don't you think he looks intelligent?"

"I do." His mother cast a critical glance over the black and white collie pups, clustered round their mother, who licked Will's outstretched hand. "Very impressive, and a good build; he'll grow up to be a fine dog. I remember Ewen Brodie said he was looking for a good sheepdog. This chap could be just the one for him."

Will's face fell. "I thought we might keep this one; he's got so used to me. I'd even thought of a name for him. What do you think of —"

Meg interrupted her son. "Now, Will, what have I said to you about getting too attached to the animals? You've always known that these puppies were going to new homes."

Will stroked the puppy's warm fur. He felt the usual pang of disappointment at his mother's detached attitude. She was always so businesslike, no time for emotion. But that was why the farm was such a success, so she must be right. He'd have one more try, though.

He stood up. "Remember you said that if I kept getting good marks at school you'd maybe let me keep one of them? Well, the marks are good, aren't they? My last report was the best yet, you said so yourself."

He turned away as he spoke, not wanting to let his mother see his expression. He was sure he was colouring up because he knew he was guilty of a fraud and he hated deceiving his mother. Tensely, he waited for her reply.

She laughed. "That's a fair comment, Will, and, yes, I must say you seem to have turned over a new leaf at school. Especially as regards your maths. Mr McDonald said that your work recently has been of a very high standard. Actually, he told me you must have really been wasting your time up to now."

Will scowled. Trust old McDonald to find an opportunity to do him down! He said nothing, and Meg went on.

"A bargain's a bargain, I suppose, so, all right, Will, I think you can look on that puppy as yours. I'll tell Mr Brodie that the one with the white nose is spoken for. How's that?"

"Oh, Ma! Thank you!"

Will gathered up the little animal and held it. He could feel its heart beating against his hand as he cradled it tenderly against his chest.

"But remember," his mother went on, "now that you've shown what you are capable of I expect the good marks to continue. You know it's important, son. It's what your father would have wanted."

Will started to say something but a cry from the yard interrupted him. "Mistress Fraser! Will you have a look at the stirk that's ailin'? Andy wants to know will we send for the vet?"

"I'm coming." Hastily Meg went outside, leaving Will alone with the little family of collies. He knelt down and put the pup back with its mother, his thoughts troubled. A sentence came into his mind, one that he remembered having to write over and over in his best writing: "Oh, what a tangled web we weave, when first we practise to deceive!"

Well, it was true enough. At the time it had seemed so easy to let Jeannie Duncan help him with his schoolwork, and, truth to tell, all the credit for the good marks should go to her. He had promised himself that it was only a short-term thing, so that his mother would let him have the puppy, but now she seemed to be expecting him to go on getting high grades. Which meant carrying on asking for Jeannie's help.

He felt bad about it. Jeannie had more than enough to do as it was. A new and ghastly thought came to him; she might well refuse to help him any more, and then what would happen? Maybe his mother would insist on selling the pup after all.

He groaned. He couldn't see any satisfactory way out.

Then a shadow fell across him, and he looked up to find Jeannie standing behind him. She had just been collecting the eggs and carried a basketful balanced on her hip. "Mornin', Master Will."

"Don't call me that!" Will stood up. "Just Will is fine, I told you."

In answer Jeannie silently inclined her head, and Will, looking past her, saw Ina standing in the doorway. He hoped she hadn't heard.

She came into the barn with a hostile glance for Jeannie. "What're you doing here, wasting your time? Those eggs should be in the dairy by now."

"I had a message for Master Will from his mother," Jeannie replied quietly. "She wants him to ride down to the village and get the vet. One of the beasts is needing attention."

"Right, I'll do that." Glad of the excuse to get away, Will hurried out into the yard to fetch his bike. Jeannie went over to the house with the basket of eggs, but Ina followed him.

"You're gettin' on fine with yon Duncan lassie, Master Will." Will stared at her, shocked by her insolent tone. She stared straight back, unblinking. "Aye, and I mind the other mornin' when I met you skulkin' down the stair from the maids' rooms —"

"Now, look here!" Will began, outraged at the turn the conversation was taking.

"Oh, so you'll have a very good reason for being up there," Ina said challengingly. "And I'm sure as the mistress would be pleased to hear it."

Will said nothing. His heart sank as he imagined his mother's response to Ina's piece of information. Jeannie would be out for sure. Even if his mother believed his story — and Ina quite plainly had other ideas — she would have no time for a servant who was not carrying out her duties efficiently. Meg Fraser was well known as a strict employer.

And worse still, the whole story of Jeannie's involvement with Will's schoolwork might come out, thereby getting both of them into even more trouble. Oh, what a tangled web, Will thought wretchedly.

"Ina," he began desperately, "it's not what you think, it really isn't. But —"

"Oh, so there'd be no harm in letting the mistress know what I saw? I can tell her all about it, then?"

"No!" The word burst from Will with more force than he intended, and he saw a look of triumph cross Ina's round face. "No," he went on more quietly, "it would be better not to mention it. If you'd be so kind."

It took him an effort to speak so civilly, when what he really wanted to do was shove Ina bodily into the nearest dung heap. She smiled at him.

"Oh, I can be kind, Master Will. If you can." The smile broadened. "You see, my Andy and me, we're hoping to be wed soon, and you know how expensive things are. If you could see your way to helping us out —"

Will felt the anger rising in him, but he knew there was nothing he could do. Furiously he dug in his pocket and brought out two half crowns, all that remained of his allowance. "Here, take that! It's all I've got. And fair's fair, not a word! Remember!"

Ina pocketed the silver. "Oh, I'll remember, Master Will. For a while at any rate."

54

Meg felt a familiar stab of apprehension as she held the telegram in her hand. She hated telegrams. They brought back all too clearly the memory of that other telegram, the one that had shattered her world when it announced Alistair's death.

She sat down at the table and opened the envelope, afraid of what it might contain. Bad news of Isobel, perhaps. Concern for her daughter, working at the military hospital in France, was ever at the back of her mind.

Taking a deep breath, she opened the envelope and scanned its contents. The next minute she was on her feet, filled with exultation.

"Will! Isobel's coming home on leave! And she's catching the sleeper; she'll be here tomorrow morning!"

Feet clattered down the stairs and the next moment Will rushed into the room. "Tomorrow! That's quick! How did she manage that?"

"She was already in London when she sent the telegram. She mentions a letter, but we never got that. Never mind. I do hope the train doesn't get delayed. Oh, Will, isn't this wonderful news?"

Will hugged his mother, and she blinked back the tears. Tears of happiness, because it was so long since she had seen her daughter. They would have so much to talk about.

At that thought a shadow came across Meg's mind. There was that marriage business. Isobel had never replied to her letter advising caution. Maybe she'd never received it. Meg remembered hearing how a mail ship had recently been torpedoed in the Channel, and it had happened before. Her letter to Isobel might be at the bottom of the sea by now. Why, for all she knew the wedding might already have taken place; Isobel was over twenty-one. Maybe her new husband was travelling with her? She might be coming as Mrs David Falconer.

Surely not! It was hardly the sort of thing one kept as a surprise. Resolutely Meg pushed the idea from her mind. Practical details had to be attended to first, like making sure a bed was aired and there was a good meal ready. Isobel deserved a comfortable, restful few days, and no doubt she would discuss her wedding plans as and when she saw fit. There was even the possibility the whole idea had been abandoned; she hadn't mentioned it in her telegram. Meg found herself beginning to feel optimistic.

She could hardly contain her excitement as she stood, early the next morning, on the platform at Aberdeen station. She'd insisted on driving the trap in herself, even though she knew it would cause a few raised eyebrows when one of the men could do it. But she begrudged every moment spent away from her daughter.

As the train drew in and the carriage doors opened, she scanned the passengers eagerly, looking for Isobel's familiar face. And there she was — Oh, but she looked so pale! And so much thinner!

Isobel saw her at the same moment and, dropping her bags, she rushed into her mother's arms. "Mother, oh, how wonderful to see you!"

Meg was choked with emotion. "Darling, you look so tired! I can't wait to get you home and feed you up. Or maybe you'll want to go and have a rest. Did you sleep much on the train?"

"Of course I did!" Isobel grinned. "Believe me, Mother, that rattly train compartment was paradise compared to some of the places I've had to try to sleep over the last year. I've got very good at just dropping off whenever the opportunity arises. What I would really love is a good big breakfast. And where's my little brother, by the way?"

"He's looking after the trap." Meg linked arms with her daughter and together, chatting happily, they walked out to where Will was waiting. He jumped down as he saw them.

"Let me give you a hand with that, Sis."

"I can manage, thanks." Isobel hefted her bag into the trap. "My, how you've grown, little brother. You must be half a head taller than me at least."

"More if you take your shoes off," Will said proudly. "And you must let me show you my puppy. And Dr Jim's going to get a motor car —"

"Really?" Isobel sounded aghast.

"It's not definite," Meg said. "His son's involved with a garage in Aberdeen; he's trying to persuade Dr Jim to get a car. Can't see it happening myself. Anyway, let's get you home and fed."

Later, after she had seen Isobel eat a hearty meal of porridge followed by eggs and home-cured bacon, Meg made an exception for once and did not go out to oversee the morning's work on the farm. They could get along without her for one day, she decided; it was far more important to spend time with Isobel, who only had three days to spend with them. Will was packed off unwillingly to school and mother and daughter sat down together in the parlour. Meg had lit a small fire as the weather was cold and overcast.

"I've got so much to tell you," Isobel said, leaning back in her armchair. "I don't know where to start. It's hard work out in France, but I can't tell you how rewarding it is. When this war is over — and please God it's soon — I'd like to train to be a proper nurse."

"But you are a proper nurse!" Meg protested. "From what you've been saying you do the same work —"

"Ooh, if Sister Marchmont could hear you, she'd have a fit! No, I'm a VAD, the lowest form of life. We're only allowed to do nursing because they are so short of trained staff. I've even been changing dressings — and, oh, Mother, the men are so brave! Sometimes it's agony for them to have the dressings changed, but they are so patient about it. I've almost been in tears myself many a time."

"You must see some harrowing sights," Meg commented.

"Yes," Isobel agreed quietly. "Even David finds it hard to take sometimes — Oh, Mother, I must tell you about David. I promised him I'd tell you all about him, so you'll love him nearly as much as I do."

So it's not over then, Meg thought to herself. It was foolish of me to think it might be. And she can't have got my letter.

"Isobel," she began, "have you really thought about things?"

But Isobel wasn't listening. She was rummaging in her bag with a worried expression. "Oh, please don't say I've left it on the train! I know I have it somewhere. Oh, here it is. Let me introduce you to your future son-in-law." With a flourish she brought out a photograph and passed it over to Meg, who, after a very slight hesitation, took it from her.

When she looked at it, Meg's heart lurched. Her eyes met the steady gaze of a dark-haired young man in military uniform, standing in a slightly self-conscious pose by a small table. His face, with its wide mouth and firm chin, was familiar to her, as was the lock of hair that fell across his high forehead, even though she had never seen Captain David Falconer before in her life. Emotion welled up in her. Why, she thought, there could be no denying whose son he was; he's the image of his father at that age!

Memories came flooding back, overwhelming in their sudden poignancy. Her hand shook as she passed the photograph back, but thankfully Isobel seemed not to notice.

"Do you like him, Mother?" she asked anxiously.

For a moment Meg couldn't trust herself to speak, but at last she managed, "It's hard to judge from a photograph, dear, but he looks a fine young man."

She got up and poked the fire, not wanting Isobel to see her expression. Tears blinded her eyes; still with her back to Isobel she pulled out a handkerchief and blew her nose. Her usually rigid self-control was deserting her.

"Mother, are you all right?"

She heard Isobel's anxious voice behind her and with a mumbled excuse she got up and left the room. Hardly knowing what she was doing she hurried upstairs to her bedroom and sat down on the bed. Her shoulders shook with the effort of holding back the tears; she buried her face in her hands.

It seemed like an eternity, but it can only have been a few minutes before she felt a hand on her shoulder, then Isobel came to sit beside her and put an arm round her. They sat in silence for a while, then Isobel said quietly. "I'm sorry, Mother. It was selfish of me to show you that photo just like that. I know it must bring back memories."

Meg turned to her daughter, her eyes searching her face. What did she mean? Had David been telling her what had happened all those years ago, before she was born?

But Isobel went on: "I know you must be thinking of Dad. You must miss him so much. I know I do." Her eyes filled with tears. "But I know you'll like David, and I hope that he can be some comfort to you, though nobody could replace Dad." She took Meg's hand and squeezed it as they both sat in silence.

At last Isobel got up. "I'd like some fresh air. I think I'll go out for a walk round the farm. Do you want to come?"

Meg shook her head. "I'll just sit here for a while, darling. I'll be down shortly."

She waited until she heard Isobel's footsteps on the stairs, then she stood up and walked over to a little writing desk in a corner of the room. With a key that hung on a fine chain round her neck, she opened the drawer and took out a faded photograph.

Apart from the differences in dress and pose, the man in this photo was almost identical to Isobel's David. A handwritten inscription in one corner read: "To my dearest Meg, all my love, now and always, James."

Meg gazed down at the photo, brittle now with age. James Falconer, the man she should have married all those years ago. And the reason why she so profoundly hoped that Isobel would never marry his son.

CHAPTER
FIVE

"You'll take a wee cuppie, Doctor?" the young crofter asked. "Tea? Or maybe a drop of something stronger?" Dr Jim, up to the elbows in an enamel bowl of hot water, returned the young man's broad grin. "A hot cup of tea will be fine, Archie, and a wee drop of whisky in it would go down very well this cold morning."

From up the stairs of the small croft cottage came the sound of a newborn baby's cry; both men listened attentively. "That's a good pair of lungs your son has, Archie. He'll make a fine young man."

"Thanks to you, Dr Jim. He wouldn't have made it without your help."

There was some truth in that, the doctor thought, as he dried his hands on a threadbare towel, then sipped his whisky-laced tea. It had been a long labour and a difficult one for Archie's young wife, and he wished she could have had the delivery in hospital where there would have been equipment and staff to make things easier. But the combined efforts of himself and Archie's mother-in-law had achieved success in the end, though it had been a close-run thing.

No point in dwelling on that though. He turned to Archie and raised his teacup in a toast. "To the young man. Have you a name for him?"

Archie turned round from coaxing the peat fire into life. "He'll take my name, just as I took my father's."

"To young Archie then." There was silence for a while as the room began to warm up. Outside, the dawn was just beginning to break, and Dr Jim knew that the young father would soon have to be at work despite having had little or no sleep. Crofting was a hard business and no respecter of events such as the arrival of a new baby. There were beasts to be fed and milked, the never-ending routine of work on the land. He decided to be off and let Archie have a little time with his wife and new son before the day's work took him away.

"I'd better be going, lad. For aught I know there might be more folk clamouring for my attention. Don't hesitate to call by if you need me."

"Thanks, Doctor."

Archie pressed some coins into Dr Jim's palm — small recompense for a night's hard work, but the doctor knew it was as much as the young man could afford — and went out into the thin rain to help harness up the pony. A few minutes later Dr Jim set off, well wrapped up in mackintosh and scarf, hunching his shoulders against the cold.

Perhaps his son Donald was right, he thought, grimacing as a flurry of fine drizzle dashed into his face. Perhaps he really ought to invest in a motor car. Then he could sit inside in comfort, away from the worst of the weather; no need to expect poor Nellie the pony to turn out in these conditions. Why, he could be almost halfway home by now! He winced at a stab of pain from his bad hip; cold weather really seemed to make it worse. People seemed to think that he, as a doctor, ought to be able to do something about it, but he knew that it was simply a case of old age. The joint was wearing out and that was that.

He thought of his son as the trap rattled along. Much to everyone's surprise, Donald seemed to be making a go of this garage business in Aberdeen. They had sold a couple of cars in their first week and were building up a list of customers needing their vehicles serviced or repaired. Maybe Donald had found his niche at last.

The doctor reached the main road and turned on to it. Not much further now, and Ellen would have a hot bath waiting, and then a warm bed for him to fall into. Please God there were no more call-outs! He didn't think he could cope if there were: it was only the rain driving into his face that was keeping him from falling asleep where he sat.

I'm getting too old for this, he thought. I need a partner, or maybe someone to take over entirely. Or maybe not that, not yet. I'm good for a few more years if only I didn't have to do all the night-time call-outs.

The rain seemed to be easing now. He let his hands rest on his lap, holding the reins loosely, and Nellie took her own pace. She knew the way from here, she'd done it often enough. Dr Jim's head fell forward; he began to nod.

The next moment a horn blared and tyres squealed. Dr Jim awoke abruptly to the sound of screeching brakes. He felt the trap being shunted sideways; Nellie reared in terror. He was falling; he made a grab at the side of the trap, but his hand closed on empty air. He hit the ground hard, felt a tremendous blow on the side of his head, and then he remembered nothing more.

"Good heavens, isn't that Mr Grant from Overton coming up to the front door?" Isobel said, looking out of the window. "And all dressed up too. I wonder what he wants? Does he often come round so early?"

Meg closed her eyes momentarily. A visit from Dod Grant was the last thing she wanted. And so early in the morning, for heaven's sake. The breakfast things were scarcely cleared away. She'd wanted to speak to the foreman too, and make sure he knew which drainage ditches she wanted clearing. Then she would have been able to let the workers get on with their work while she spent precious time with her daughter.

Now it looked as though everything would be set back. The men would be waiting for her to give them their orders for the day and so much time would be wasted. She'd hoped they might just about get those ditches finished today, but now it looked doubtful.

And knowing Dod Grant, he'd probably want to talk at length about the proposed merger of the two farms. With Isobel being at home there hadn't been time for Meg to think things through, and she knew from experience that you had to be sure of your ground before you got into negotiating with Dod Grant. He was a wily customer and no mistake, one who drove a hard bargain. The more she thought about it, the more she decided she would have to put him off. Offer him a quick cup of tea and arrange another time for their discussion. It would be after she'd had a chance to speak to the solicitor and make sure that her own interests — and, more importantly, Will's — were fully protected.

"Mother?" Isobel prompted. "Is everything all right? Why is Mr Grant here?"

"He's probably come about farm business," Meg answered vaguely. "But I'll ask him to arrange another visit. I want to spend time with you today. And yes, he thinks nothing of visiting first thing in the morning. He believes in being up with the lark, if not before, and all credit to him. He's not afraid of hard work."

"It's paid off too, from what I hear," Isobel said. "Somebody was telling me he's frightfully prosperous these days. Not that you'd think it to look at him. Anyway, I'd better go and leave you to it."

"No, don't go." Meg put out a hand to her daughter. "If you're here it will surely make him understand that it's not a good time to talk business. Anyway, I'm sure he'd be interested to see you too after all this time."

Isobel laughed. "Anyone would think you wanted me as your chaperon!"

Meg stared at her for a moment, then she laughed too. "I shouldn't think anyone ever needed a chaperon to protect them from Dod Grant! I doubt that any thought of romance has ever crossed his mind."

"You never know," Isobel teased. "Wouldn't it be funny if he had been harbouring a secret passion for you all these years?"

Meg flinched; that comment was too close for comfort. Recently that very thought had passed through her own mind, only to be firmly rejected. She flashed her daughter a mock scowl. "Oh yes, very funny, I'm sure. The whole neighbourhood would be helpless with mirth. But I'm the last person anyone could harbour a secret passion for — even Dod Grant. You surely know that I'm a byword for unfeminine behaviour, running a farm, not afraid to get my hands dirty. Romance doesn't enter into it."

There was a short silence, then Isobel said, "But it wasn't always like that, was it? Dad fell in love with you."

"That was a long time ago," Meg said brusquely. "A lot has changed since then. But we're keeping poor old Dod waiting. Let's find out what he wants then we can get on with the rest of the day." She spoke to Jeannie, who had just come through to clear away the last of the breakfast things. "Ask Mr Grant to step through, will you, Jeannie?"

A few moments later Dod came in, twisting his flat cap between his fingers. He looked nonplussed when he saw Meg had company.

"Miss Isobel!" He recovered swiftly. "Glad to see you home again — for good, is it?"

"No, Mr Grant." Isobel shook hands. "Only three days' leave, I'm afraid, then I'm off back. I hope you're well?"

"Never better, lassie, never better." He shot a quick glance at Meg as he spoke. "So your mother will have been telling you about our plans, then, eh?"

Seeing her daughter's look of enquiry, Meg rushed into speech. "I hadn't got round to telling you anything yet, Isobel. Mr Grant has been suggesting we might join our two farms. Together they would make a more economic unit, and there'd be scope for a lot of improvements that wouldn't be worthwhile on a smaller property."

"I see." Isobel sounded doubtful, and Meg observed her giving Dod Grant an appraising stare. Quite clearly she wasn't impressed by the thought of him as her mother's business partner.

Adopting what she hoped was a light conversational tone, Meg asked, "What brings you over here so early, Mr Grant? Will you take some refreshment, by the way?"

"Just a spot of tea would be fine, mistress, thankee. Aye, I brought that bantam cockerel over, the one we were speakin' about."

"We were?"

"Aye, we were. I'm glad to give you the loan of him for a whiley."

"I'll go and see to the tea," Isobel said, and was gone before Meg could stop her. As if on cue, Dod hitched his chair closer to Meg's.

"A right bonnie lass, that daughter of yours," he commented approvingly.

"You think so?"

"Aye, that I do." He twirled the end of his sparse moustache. "But she's not a patch on her mother."

Meg swallowed hard. She had to dig her nails into her palms to stop herself from laughing out loud as the memory of Isobel's joking comments came back to her. So Dod really was trying a little gallantry to try to soften her up! She would never have believed it possible, but she'd make it quite plain he wouldn't get anywhere with that sort of approach.

Deliberately she kept the conversation about Isobel. "Isobel isn't looking her best at the moment. She's only just home, and the conditions out in France are grim."

"They are, right enough," Dod agreed. "In the medical line, she is, that right?"

"Yes, she's a VAD."

"Very good, very good. You'll be proud of her, I don't doubt." He cleared his throat. "There was something I wanted to ask you, mistress, or maybe I could presume on our old acquaintance and call you Meg? If it's not taking too much liberty?"

"Well, I —" Meg felt distinctly irritated. This patronizing behaviour was just too much! In another moment, she felt, she would lose all sense of politeness and tell Dod Grant exactly what she thought of him. But no, she would have to bite her tongue. Will's future prospects might depend on this deal. If only something would happen to get her out of this situation before her hasty temper ruined everything!

And then, suddenly, shockingly, her wish was realized. The door burst open and Isobel came hurrying in.

"Mother, Mr Grant, I'm sorry to disturb you but something dreadful has happened. Dr Nicol has had an accident!"

"What! How?" Meg shot to her feet, appalled. She felt almost as though she had wished this mishap, whatever it was, on Dr Jim.

"He was driving home in his trap from a visit early this morning before it was properly light, and a motor car ran into the back of him."

"Oh no, how terrible!" Meg's hand flew to her mouth. "How is he? Is he badly hurt?"

"He was thrown out and knocked unconscious, and he's injured his leg. The poor man lay helpless in a ditch until someone came by and found him. Donald's here; he's asked me to go over and see if I could help. Do you mind if I go?"

"Of course not!" Meg said decisively. "In fact, I'll come too. I don't have your medical expertise, but I hope I could be some use to Ellen."

She turned to her visitor. "Mr Grant, you must excuse me. I can't sit here and do nothing. I must go and see Dr Jim straight away. His wife's a good friend of mine. Do stay and take your cup of tea —"

"Nay, mistress, if you're not taking one I won't either." Dod had stood up too. "I had hoped for a wee word wi' ye, but I can see your mind's on other things. Some other time."

"Yes, some other time," Meg echoed. She was hardly noticing what she was saying, her thoughts were all on the Nicols. Poor Dr Jim, and poor Ellen! She must be out of her mind with worry.

CHAPTER
SIX

"It could have been a lot worse." Isobel sat down with her mother and Dr Jim's wife, Ellen. "He's had a lucky escape."

"So you don't think there's anything broken?" Ellen asked.

"No, not as far as I can tell, and he doesn't either. But his left leg is very stiff, and he's in a lot of pain."

"That's his bad hip," Ellen said worriedly. "He's always had trouble with it and this is bound to make it worse."

"He'll have to keep to his bed for a while and rest it," Meg put in. "And convincing him of that won't be easy, Ellen. In a way it would have been simpler if he'd had to be put in plaster."

Ellen gave her a rueful smile. "Doctors don't tend to make good patients at the best of times, and my Jim was never blessed with much patience. I'm not sure what I'm going to do, Meg. Short of tying him down in the bed —"

"Perhaps I should have a word with him," Meg suggested. "He might take advice better from an outsider."

"Hardly an outsider — you're an old friend! But it can't hurt. The more people who try to convince him to stay put until he's properly healed the better."

"How is he?" Meg asked Isobel. "I don't want to disturb him if he's sleeping."

Isobel laughed. "Sleeping? Him? No, I left him fretting about how soon he was going to get back on his rounds. He was talking about coming downstairs this afternoon."

"Oh no! What shall I do?" Ellen started to get up. "Once he's made his mind up he's so difficult to argue with."

"I'll go and talk to him right now," Meg offered. "I'm sure I can get him to see sense."

Ellen looked doubtful but made no objection, so Meg left the room and made her way up the stairs to the room where Dr Jim lay. She heard his voice as she approached the door. He was arguing with his son.

"Look here, Donald, there's no point you going on about what might have happened. It didn't, and that's that. I'm perfectly well apart from a bit of stiffness, and I'm not prepared to let that interfere with my doing my job. There are people out there depending on me."

Meg knocked at the door before Donald could reply. She put her head round. "Good morning, Jim, I'm pleased to hear you in such good voice. How's the patient, Donald?"

Donald flashed her a relieved smile. "Very impatient as you can hear. We're going to have our work cut out persuading him to take things easy."

A snort came from the bed. "There's nothing wrong with me, apart from a few bruises. Stop treating me like an invalid."

Meg sat down next to the bed. She could see that although her old friend was putting a brave face on things, there were lines of pain etched into his face and he bit down hard on his lower lip as he tried to sit up.

"Jim," she said quietly, "there's no shame in admitting you're human. You've had a shake-up, and the best thing you can do is take the time you need to get over it —"

"Don't you lecture me, Meg Fraser!" The doctor wagged a stern finger at her. "You're the last person to give in to things. Remember that time you insisted on sitting up all night with a sick horse when you were going down with bronchitis?"

"Yes, but —"

"But nothing! If I'm in my bed, who's to see to my patients? Tell me that now!"

Meg was prepared for this. She'd discussed it with Donald and Isobel on the way over. "One of the doctors from town could see to them for a while. I'm sure someone would be prepared to help out. Dr Harrison maybe."

"Harrison? That old fool! I wouldn't let him anywhere near any of my patients!"

"How about that young Dr Mclean?"

"Still wet behind the ears!"

Meg suppressed a sigh. "Well, I'm sure we'll find someone to take over for a while. It's important that you get some rest, and I'm going to make sure you do."

"Oh yes?" Dr Jim challenged. "And how do you propose to do that? What's going to stop me getting out of this bed as soon as your back's turned?"

In reply, Meg turned to his son. "Donald, could you collect all your father's pairs of trousers for me? I'm sure some of them need a bit of mending, and while he's indisposed would be a good time to do it."

Donald stared at her for a moment, then his face split into a broad grin. "Certainly, Mrs Fraser. I'll do that right now."

"Thank you. Now, Jim, I'd better be getting home. I've a farm to run. But I'll take your clothes with me, just to be on the safe side."

If looks could kill she would have been dead on the floor. But she made it safely out of the room and down the stairs, where she told a horrified Ellen what she'd done.

"Oh, Meg! How could you? It's true what they say — you're a very determined woman."

Meg laughed. "It was the only way I could think of to make sure he stayed put. But don't you get soft-hearted and give him something to wear."

"I won't," Ellen promised. "You'd never forgive me, I know." She changed the subject. "While you were upstairs Isobel was telling me about her wedding plans. How thrilling that she wants to be married from Braehead."

"Oh." This was news to Meg. She stared blankly at Isobel, who coloured up.

"Mother and I haven't had much chance to talk yet," Isobel explained to Ellen. "But I expect that's what you would want too, isn't it?" she appealed to Meg.

Meg said nothing for a while. She felt very guilty that in the twenty-four hours or so that Isobel had been home they hadn't made time to discuss the wedding plans. In fact, to be honest, she'd shied away from the subject, subconsciously hoping against hope that the event might never happen. But it would have to be faced up to, and soon.

"Yes, of course," she said, with some semblance of enthusiasm. "But it won't be for a while yet."

To her great relief, Isobel agreed. "No, not till the war is over, and please God that's soon. If we married before then I couldn't carry on with my work, and David agrees it's important that I do. He's just as keen as I am that we should be married up here in the parish church. His family are looking forward to coming up; none of them has been to Scotland before."

Meg found a smile from somewhere, as Ellen and Isobel chatted about the wedding.

She wondered just how much Isobel really did know. She couldn't know the whole story, or surely she would have reacted with horror. Probably David didn't know either. He would certainly have told Isobel if he did. But if there was to be a big wedding with both families present, then everything would be bound to come out. What would Isobel say then? What would she think of her mother?

And, most difficult of all, Meg thought depressingly, I will have to face James again after all these years. How am I going to do it?

* * *

"The square on the hypotenuse of a right-angled triangle," Will repeated without enthusiasm, "is equal to the sum of the squares on the other two sides. That's right, isn't it?"

"Yes, well done," Jeannie Duncan congratulated him. "So you see, you can easily work out the length of this side of the triangle if you know the other two. Try this one."

Will picked up a pencil and applied himself to his exercise book. It was quiet up in the hayloft, just the two of them sitting on old packing cases. From down below them came the cluck of hens scratching in the yard and the occasional low of one of the beasts in the byre.

"Hurry up and finish," Jeannie urged. "I need to be back in the kitchen to make the brose. Ina will be out looking for me if I'm not in soon."

"Nearly there." Will chewed the end of his pencil while he wrestled with a calculation in his head. "I say, Jeannie, what's the point of all this?"

"What do you mean?"

"I mean why do I need to know about right-angled triangles when I'm going to be a farmer? What's the use of it? I can't see that there is any."

Jeannie frowned at him. "You sound just like my brother Sandy. Surely you will want folk to know you're an educated man? And you need to know your arithmetic to see you're not being cheated —"

"I know that. But these triangles, what use are they? And history, and geography — what have they to do with running a farm?"

76

Jeannie was silent for a moment, then she turned away. Will was convinced that he'd upset her; he threw down his pencil and went over to where she sat. "I'm sorry. I'm not meaning to say that I don't appreciate what you're doing for me. You're a great help, really you are. You explain things so well, you make it all so clear."

He was appalled to see a tear glistening on her cheek, and almost put out a hand to wipe it away. Just in time he thought better of it, and instead pulled out a handkerchief. "Here, take this. It's clean."

"Thanks." Jeannie's voice was muffled. She wiped her eyes and managed a watery smile. "Sorry, it's silly of me to get like this —"

"No, it's my fault. I shouldn't have said what I did."

Jeannie got up and walked to the cobwebby window of the hayloft, looking out into the farmyard, away from Will. "You can't help how you feel," she said at last. "And I can't help it that I want an education but I can't have one. I'd jump at the chance of what you've got, Will, and you seem so ready to throw it away. It makes me angry."

Will felt ashamed. "It's not fair, is it? Both of us pushed into doing what we don't want to do."

"But that's life. I can't help it that my mother needs me to go out to work and earn money. You can't help it that your mother is ambitious for you. We've both got to make the best of things. In time things will change; you'll be in charge of this farm and I'll get to train as a teacher."

"You really think you will?"

Defiantly, she turned to face him. "Of course I will! It's the only thing that keeps me going! When Ina is horrible to me, when I have to get up at five on a freezing cold morning and light the fire, when I don't get to my bed until midnight because I've been trying to study — then I think to myself, someday, *someday* I'll be able to put all this behind me."

Will was impressed. At the same time he felt troubled that Jeannie was so obviously unhappy. "Listen, Jeannie, why don't you speak to my mother about Ina? Or perhaps I could say something?"

"Don't you dare! She'd think I'd been moaning to you; she'd never believe it. No, I want to do things my way. I don't need your help. Now I'd better be going before Ina comes looking for me."

So saying, she picked up the couple of books she'd brought with her and began to climb down the ladder from the loft. Will watched her go in silence.

He wished he could do something to help her, but she was right. Any interference from him would simply make matters worse. She didn't need him at all, but he needed her. With her tuition he was making much better progress at school and his mother was delighted. All down to Jeannie's patient help. She'd make a fine teacher, he acknowledged.

He stuffed the exercise book in his pocket and, after glancing through the window to check that Jeannie was out of sight, he climbed down the ladder. He paused to visit the collie pups then he too crossed the yard to the house. As he approached the kitchen door, it opened, and to his dismay Ina came out.

Will increased his pace to avoid her but she came towards him and his heart sank. Had she seen him and Jeannie together?

It looked like his fears were confirmed by the smirk on Ina's round face. "Mornin', Master Will, been seein' your young lady again?"

"I don't know what you mean," Will began, but she interrupted him.

"Oh, I know what's goin' on. And I'm shocked, really I am. To think of you, the son of the house takin' advantage of a poor servant girl —"

"Now look here! It's not like that at all!"

"Really? Secret meetings in the hayloft? Whatever could you be doin' up there? I'm minded that I should have a word with the mistress about it."

"No, don't do that." Will felt the grip of desperation. "Please."

"Well, I could be persuaded —" Ina began slyly.

"All right." Will felt in his pocket for some coins, the money he'd been going to use for a new fishing rod. Something would have to be done about this, he thought grimly as he handed the money over to a grinning Ina. But he really couldn't think what.

CHAPTER
SEVEN

"Mistress Fraser, how good to see you again." The elderly solicitor stood up politely as Meg entered his office. "Do take a seat. I hear your daughter is home on leave. How is she getting on in France? Terribly dangerous, especially for a young girl, but we all admire her for serving her country — so very courageous. And they tell me she is to be married. It seems congratulations are in order."

Not for the first time, Meg marvelled at how quickly news spread in Aberdeen. For a bustling city it was surprisingly parochial.

"Yes, you're quite right, Mr Wishart." Summoning up a smile, she described something of Isobel's work in France, and made brief reference to the proposed marriage. "But I mustn't be too long," she finished, "Isobel has so little time with us."

"Of course, of course. She's in town with you?"

"No, she's visiting an old school friend this afternoon."

"I see. So what can I do for you, Mistress Fraser?"

Meg took a deep breath. "I wanted to speak to you about a suggestion that has been made to me about merging Braeside with a neighbouring farm."

Mr Wishart looked at her over his half-moon spectacles. "Ah. And would that neighbouring farm be Overton, by any chance?"

Meg smiled to herself. There was little that the solicitor did not miss. "Yes, it would. I have more or less decided what I want to do, but I wanted to discuss the legal side of things with you."

He leaned back in his chair, steepling the tops of his fingers together. At last he said, "It's difficult to say without knowing the details, but in principle I would think it a sound move, Mistress Fraser. It would make a large property, but thinking of the future, of mechanization, of labour costs, joining the two properties would be an advantage. You could have a very thriving business there. But I expect you have already thought these things through?"

"I have, though not in any detail as yet."

"So the suggestion has been made by Mr Grant?"

"It has. At first I was unsure, but the more I think about it the more I feel it would be a good thing. Especially for Will."

"Ah yes. Mr Grant is a bachelor, I understand."

"Yes, he's never married, and at his age I shouldn't think he has any plans to do so, so it could be that Will would eventually take over the two farms. This is something we would have to agree to between us. I must say that Will's future was uppermost in my mind when I agreed to consider the matter. I owe it to my late husband's memory to do the best I possibly can for our son."

"Indeed. I admire you very much for your hard work in building up the business so far. Many people shook their heads when you decided to run Braeside on your own, but you've proved them all wrong. Your son is getting a very good start in life thanks to you."

"Thank you, I appreciate that." Meg smiled at the elderly man. "Everything I do is with Will in mind. And Isobel, of course, though it looks as though she has her own future mapped out. So," she continued, "we would need to draw up a watertight agreement with Mr Grant and his solicitors. Both sides need to know where they stand so there could be no cause for disagreement later."

"We can certainly do that, Mistress Fraser. You are right to be prudent. Mr Grant is well known as — shall we say — a shrewd businessman."

Meg nodded. "I've had dealings with him before, and I have managed to fight my corner. But obviously I have no legal training, so I need you to deal with that side of things."

"Of course. You may depend upon that, Mistress Fraser. It should all be very straightforward."

"Good."

Meg stayed a while longer discussing some of the detail, then at last she went out into the fresh outside air. The late afternoon was turning cold and she looked forward to getting home to tea and toast by the fireside with Isobel.

When she eventually arrived home, however, it was not to find Isobel waiting by the fire but a very different person.

82

"It's Mr Grant, ma'am," Jeannie Duncan told her. "He's here on more business, he says."

Good grief, Meg thought to herself, as she took off her hat and coat. He hasn't wasted much time. I wonder if he heard I was at the solicitor's this afternoon. Anyway, best go and speak to him about it.

She summoned up a polite smile as she went into the parlour and greeted him.

"Good evening, Mr Grant. How the nights are drawing in! It makes you glad to be by the fireside."

"Aye, I'm thinking the weather's set to turn for the worse."

He sat down opposite her by the fire and a silence descended, broken only by Jeannie bringing in a tray of tea and scones. Meg poured the tea and put the plate of scones by Dod Grant, who took one. She herself felt no hunger at all. Silence yawned again.

At last Meg could stand it no longer. Isobel would be back soon; she didn't want to waste yet more time with Dod Grant. Better to arrange another time when they could have a proper discussion. "I presume you've come to talk about joining our two farms, Mr Grant. As it happens I've been to see the solicitor this afternoon and he's happy to go ahead with the arrangements as soon as you like."

"That's right good news, Mistress Fraser." Dod's thin features broke into a smile. "I'm glad to hear it, very glad. Did he happen to say how long it would take? Maybe by October?"

"I really couldn't say. It depends on how straightforward it all is. I thought you and I could usefully talk it over between us first before the legal folk get going. It could save us some money."

"Indeed it would." Dod sounded impressed. "No point in them swallowing all our profits."

"No." Meg hid a smile at Dod's legendary tightfistedness. But he seemed in a good mood; she decided to air the thought that concerned her most.

"My first thought in all this has to be for Will," she said. "He will of course take over Braehead eventually, but I wonder how you feel about the future of Overton?"

Dod bridled. "I'm good for a few years yet! I've no mind to retire! But your Will's a good lad, even though you're stuffing his head full of too much schooling in my opinion." He ignored Meg's frown, and went on, "No, I look upon your Will as the son I never had; I'd be proud to do what I can to help him on his way. Take him under my wing."

"I hardly think that would be necessary —" Meg began but Dod didn't seem to hear her.

"Maybe while the legal folk are busy on the arrangements we could ask them about formal adoption. What do you think about that? The lad needs a father —"

"*What?*" Meg frowned. She put her teacup down with a clatter. "I don't think I understand . . ."

Dod slanted her a knowing smile. "Why, after we're man and wife, of course. It's only right that the lad should have two parents, all right and proper. And that lass of yours, thinking about being wed. She'll need someone to lead her down the aisle. Don't you think so?"

Meg swallowed hard. So it had come to this after all! She could hardly believe what she was hearing. She was torn between incredulous laughter and bitter anger at his presumption. But what an idiot she'd been! How had she let things get this far?

"Mr Grant," she said at last, fighting hard for self-control, "I think there's been some misunderstanding. I — I can't remember ever having agreed to *marry* you."

It was Dod's turn to frown. "But of course you did, lass. Wasn't that the whole point of the thing?"

"The whole point?"

"Well, maybe not quite. But I thought I'd made myself clear. Why, how else could we do it? I'm not wanting a woman as a business partner, t'ain't right. No, what I'm wanting is a wife, and I know you'd make me a good 'un."

It was too much for Meg. The words poured out before she could stop them. "Marry you? You really imagined I'd marry you? What on earth must you have been thinking? Well, I'm sorry, Mr Grant, but there's nothing further from my mind. Good heavens, how did you ever presume such a thing? It's preposterous!"

Then she realized what she was saying. She was insulting the poor man; she owed him common politeness at least. Why, she thought suddenly, he might decide to abandon the whole scheme and then Will's future was at stake. She turned to face him, making herself speak calmly. "Thank you for your proposal, Mr Grant, but I'm sorry I can't accept it."

Seconds passed, and she watched the emotions cross Dod's weatherbeaten features. Disbelief, disappointment and finally anger. He glared at her.

"That's a fine way of behavin', mistress, leadin' an honest man on like that."

"Leading you on! I never did anything of the sort!"

"Well, to my mind you did. Why else would I have made the offer? If all I wanted was a bigger farm I could have asked to join with Drumlaire on the other side of the hill. Some say it's better ground than yours."

Meg was stung into a response. "I very much doubt that. Have you seen the stones they dig out of the ground there? But if that's what you want, then go ahead. I've run this farm on my own for the past three years. I can go on doing it."

"Aye, you can that. But you could do better. More land, more scope. Think about it. I know you've wanted to drain that low-lying patch, but the cost put you off. Well, it wouldn't cost much more to do that bit of mine as well, then there'd be a sizeable area ready for cultivation. Think what we could do with it. And we could afford a tractor, other machinery as well. That's the way forward, lass. Think what a grand farm we could build up for that son of yours."

Meg didn't need to think. She was well aware of what Dod described. Hadn't she thought about it herself already?

"But we could still do all that," she said, trying to be reasonable. "What's to prevent us? It's in both our interests to go ahead."

"Aye, it is, right enough. But you know my terms, and you can't say now that I haven't made myself plain. I'm offering you marriage, mistress, and it's that or nothing. What's your mind?"

He was smiling at her, Meg noticed, as if he was certain of her reply, sure that she would cave in and fall in with his plans. Her temper ignited.

"In that case," she said crisply, "the deal's off. I have no plans of marriage."

"But, but —" Dod spluttered. "What's the problem? Let me tell you, there's many a woman in this county would be glad to have me —"

"Then I suggest you go and ask them."

He drew himself up to his full height, fractionally shorter than her, and stared her in the face. "Aye, maybe I will. But I'll say this to you, mistress, the day will come when you'll be sorry you turned me down, aye, that it will. You've made a big mistake."

Scowling, he turned on his heel, slamming the door behind him. Meg stood still for a while, breathing hard, trying to control her spiralling emotions. Had she done the right thing?

At the idea of being the wife of Dod Grant, a shudder ran through her. Yes, she had definitely done the right thing there. But what of Will? She sensed she had just made an implacable enemy. What would be the consequences for her son?

Isobel was worried. Something was wrong with her mother. She had gone to bed early the previous night, complaining of a raging headache, and she really hadn't looked at all well. They couldn't send for Dr Jim — he was laid up after his accident — and Mother would not countenance sending for a doctor from town. She'd refused any help from Isobel too, saying that a good night's sleep would see her right, but in the morning she'd still been pale and somehow distracted.

"What do you think we should do?" Isobel asked Will before he set off for school. "She hasn't touched her breakfast."

"She'll be all right. She's never ill. She's probably just worried about something."

"I wish I had your confidence," Isobel said darkly. "And if she's worried about something it must be pretty bad. She looks terrible."

"It hasn't stopped her going out to speak to the foreman about ploughing," Will countered. "So she can't be that bad."

"Mother could be at death's door and she'd still make an effort to carry on as normal. You know her."

"Stop worrying! It's your last day at home and we're having that special dinner tonight. If you go around with a long face you'll upset Ma, and that won't help, will it?"

"Perhaps I should extend my leave. An illness in the family is a good enough reason."

"But she's not ill!"

Isobel gave up. But after Will had run off down the hill to catch the bus, she sat for a while, deep in thought.

If only she could speak to David. She missed him so much. Her lips curved in a smile as she pictured him, tall, dark and so heart-stoppingly good-looking in his military uniform.

She remembered the first time they'd met, in a smoky bar not far from the army hospital. Female staff weren't supposed to be there, but she and a couple of friends had sneaked off one night, desperate for a break from the harrowing round of duty. David and his friends had come over to their table, and got talking. It had been a surprise to discover that David hailed from the small town in England that Isobel knew was her mother's childhood home.

There'd been so much to talk about. She and David had sat together, oblivious of everyone around them, until they'd realized with a start that it was long after twelve and she was supposed to be on duty at six the next morning.

He'd given her a lift on the back of a motorbike, and she smiled again as she remembered that bumpy ride along the dark muddy lanes, her arms fastened tightly round his waist, her head buried in his shoulder. And he'd kissed her as they said goodbye, just briefly, but enough to convey how he felt about her.

And the rest, as they say, was history.

Meanwhile, there was the difficulty of what to do about her mother. Isobel wondered whether there was a problem with the farm. Could it be losing money? She remembered Dod Grant's visit. Perhaps there was some dispute?

"Isobel?"

She jumped at the sound of her mother's voice, but managed to keep up an appearance of unconcern as Meg popped her head round the door.

"I have to go down to the village, darling, but I won't be long. Is there anything you want from the shop?"

"Er — oh, please could you get me a few cakes of soap? It's in terrible short supply over at the hospital — well, *nice* soap. The sort they have is awful."

"Poor you. Yes, I'll get you the nicest I can find. I'll be back in about half an hour."

With that she was gone, leaving Isobel still worried. Despite the casual words, Meg looked pale and drawn, with shadow-ringed eyes that told of a sleepless night. There was definitely something wrong, and Isobel was determined to find out.

On impulse she made her way to the farm office, a small room at the back of the house. Keeping her ears open for her mother's footfall in the passageway, she quickly scanned through the paperwork on the desk.

It was all routine stuff. A quick search of the desk drawers revealed nothing that would cause Meg such anxiety. If there was some documentary evidence then it was well hidden.

Isobel sat at the desk deep in thought, then she pushed back the chair and stood up. Perhaps her mother had taken some paperwork to her room.

She went upstairs feeling very uncomfortable, but she damped down her conscience with the thought that she was trying to act in her mother's best interests.

Meg's room was cosy and peaceful, looking out over the fields to the sea, grey in the distance. Beside the bed was a photo of her late husband, and Isobel's heart lurched as she looked at it. "God bless you, Daddy," she whispered.

The room was immaculately tidy as always, no papers of any sort lying about. Isobel went over to the small writing desk that stood in a corner. If Meg had brought any documents up to her room this was surely where they would be. With a scared glance over her shoulder, Isobel tried the drawer; it was not locked.

But all it contained was a bundle of old letters tied with a ribbon, and a photograph. Isobel felt disappointed; it looked like her quest had failed. Then she looked at the photograph.

The room whirled around her; she had to clutch at the edge of the desk for support. The face that looked out at her from the old photo was one so infinitely dear to her, one that she knew so well. David's face.

But the photo must be years old. It was brittle and fading, and the inscription — She gazed at it in profound shock, not able to understand.

And then there was a figure in the doorway, a voice speaking. "Isobel, I've been looking everywhere for you. Is anything —"

Meg's voice trailed off into silence as she saw what her daughter held in her hand. Mother and daughter stood in absolute stillness while long seconds ticked by.

Then at last Meg broke the spell. "Isobel, darling — let me try to explain."

CHAPTER
EIGHT

There was silence for a few moments, broken only by the cawing of rooks outside the window, wheeling through the cold grey sky. Then Isobel said quietly, "You don't need to say anything if you don't want to. It was wrong of me to pry — I'm sorry. But I was so worried about you. I wanted to see if I could find out what was upsetting you."

"There's nothing upsetting me," Meg said, sitting down on the bed and motioning to Isobel to come and sit beside her. "Just a business matter that's on my mind at the moment. It will all be sorted out soon."

"It's Dod Grant, isn't it? That partnership idea?" Isobel grasped her mother's hand and held it tightly.

Meg sighed. "Yes, you're right. I gave it a lot of thought because in some ways it made sense. But now we've dropped the idea; we simply couldn't agree on the terms. It worried me at first, but on reflection I think it's for the best."

"I'm sure it is! He's the last person to be in partnership with. They say he's only out for himself. I'm glad you saw through him, Mother."

So am I, Meg thought to herself. If only I'd seen through him sooner! And let's hope no one else gets to hear what a fool I've made of myself. Surely Dod won't want to spread it around?

"Don't be hard on him, Isobel," she said to her daughter. "He's a very successful farmer. He's built that place up from nothing. Just because he's a bit — well, eccentric —"

"I know. But all the same I wouldn't like the thought of him being involved here. Trying to boss you around —"

Meg laughed. "I'd like to see him try! Anyway, it's not going to happen. I told him I didn't think it would work."

"Good." Isobel leaned her head on her mother's shoulder. At last she said tentatively, "But, Mother, the photograph. It's David's father, isn't it?"

"Yes." Meg thought rapidly. How much to tell Isobel? Enough to explain away the existence of the photo, she decided, but no more than was strictly necessary. Blessing the habits of quick thinking that she'd cultivated over her years of running the farm, she said, "I suppose you can guess, can't you? James and I were sweethearts, long ago. It was over, of course, by the time I met your father, but I kept the photo as a reminder of happy times."

"Oh, I see." Isobel sounded doubtful. "That's an odd coincidence, isn't it? But it's not like you to be sentimental, Mother."

"No, it isn't, is it?" Meg gave a rueful smile. How little people knew about her, even her own daughter!

They saw only the rather brusque, no-nonsense exterior; no idea of the romantic soul that she was so careful to hide. Alistair had known about James Falconer, of course, but he had never revealed her secret, bless him.

"I don't think David can know either," Isobel went on, "because he's never said anything about it."

"Probably because his father has forgotten all about me," Meg said. "We were very young at the time, and it's years ago now. I expect he never gives me a thought."

The words pained her as she said them, but she kept her tone deliberately casual. And it was probably the truth. After she'd gone to Scotland, James had made no effort to get in touch, he had simply obliterated her from his life. Whereas she had treasured that photo all these years. How foolish of me! she thought suddenly, and before Isobel could stop her she picked up the photo and ripped it in half. "There!"

"Mother, what did you do that for?" Isobel, clearly shocked, reached for the torn halves and stared down at them. "You've kept this for so long — why do you want to tear it up now?"

"Because it was silly of me to keep it. It belongs to the past." Meg felt the tears pricking at her eyelids but she blinked them back. "I was very happily married to your father. It was wrong of me to hang on to that photo."

"But Daddy could have no reason to criticize you. You've just said it was all over long before you met him. I suppose he knew about it?"

"Oh yes, I told him, of course I did. We never had any secrets from each other."

"Well, then. There was no need to tear up the photo. I'd have liked David to see it."

Meg felt a stab of alarm. "I don't think that's wise, darling. If David's father hasn't seen fit to mention anything to him —"

"I know. But don't you think he ought to know that the two of you were — well, friendly in the past? After all, you're going to meet at the wedding."

The wedding! Meg closed her eyes. She'd given up on trying to talk Isobel out of it. She knew that her daughter had inherited her own strong will, and there was no point in attempting to dissuade her from the course she'd set herself. And, in fairness, David looked an excellent young man, just the sort of husband she would have wanted for her daughter. If only he hadn't been James's son!

"I'm going to paste this back together," Isobel said, getting up with the photo in her hand. "I'll stick it on to a piece of strong paper, that'll help preserve it."

"All right. But leave it with me, will you? I promise I won't destroy it, if that's what you want."

"Thanks." Isobel gave her mother a hug then went out, leaving Meg alone. Her thoughts were busy, winging back over the years. To the outskirts of a small town in the south of England, a hillside overlooking the sea. James Falconer sitting beside her on a bench, his head in his hands, while she sat silent, tears welling up and spilling over down her face.

"I'm sorry, James, it has to be no."

"Has to be? Who says so? Why have you changed your mind?"

He raised his head and looked at her, and she caught her breath at the bitter anguish in his face.

"I — I don't think it would work —"

"Why not? We love each other, don't we? Or have you changed your mind on that as well?"

"You know I haven't."

"So?" He was silent for a few moments, then he turned away abruptly. "It's your parents, isn't it? They've turned you against me."

She took a deep calming breath. "They've refused their consent, yes. And I am under age."

"And their reason?"

"That you are a widower with a young son." It was difficult to speak, her heart was so full. "They don't think I could cope."

"Meg, we've been through all this. You get on splendidly with little David. He loves you already. And my mother is more than happy to help." He picked up a stone and sent it winging out to sea. "No, it's not that. Let's be honest, shall we? Your parents don't think I'm good enough for you. I'm from the wrong side of the tracks. Not the right family connections."

Meg said nothing. She couldn't trust herself to speak. What James was saying was the truth; it was what her parents had spelled out so clearly.

He turned round and took both her hands in his before she could pull away.

96

"Meg, what does all that matter to us? The world is changing; those sort of old-fashioned class distinctions are being swept away. You've said yourself you don't give a fig for that sort of thing. Let me talk to your parents. I'm sure I can convince them."

Meg closed her eyes, remembering her father's angry words. "No, James, it wouldn't work. My father won't give way."

"Then we'll have to wait until you're twenty-one. I won't give up. I'll wait for you, Meg."

"No! We can't, it won't —" She stopped, forcing back a sob. "There's more to it than that."

"Go on."

She bit her lip. "It — it's making my mother ill. She's always had a weak heart, and my father says that the worry of all this is bad for her. It's putting her life at risk. James, I could never forgive myself if anything happened to her because of me."

He released her hands and sat back, his eyes still on her face. "So that's what he says, is it? How very convenient."

"James!"

"Well, isn't it? I've never known your mother have a day's illness in her life, and now suddenly this!"

Meg moved away. "Are you calling my father a liar?"

"I'm saying he might be . . . exaggerating."

She pulled out a handkerchief and wiped her eyes. "In that case there's no more to be said."

There was silence for a while, and then James said quietly, "Don't let's get angry with each other. I'm sorry I said that. But there must be a way forward for us. This can't be the end."

"It has to be, James." Meg's voice was a mere thread. "I'm going away."

"*What?*"

"It's all arranged. I have an aunt in Edinburgh who's not been well. I'm going up to stay with her, as a sort of companion. I expect to be there for at least a year. I —"

James was on his feet, staring down at her. "I don't believe this!"

"I'm sorry, it's all arranged."

He reached for her hands and pulled her up. "You're telling me you agreed to all this without a word to me? That you'd already made up your mind? How the hell could you throw everything away just like that? I thought you loved me!"

"I —"

"I thought you had some strength of will! But I was mistaken, wasn't I? You daren't give up your comfortable life and take a risk on me. I'm disappointed in you, Meg."

"James, don't let's part like this. Please."

He laughed. "How did you expect us to part? Did you think I'd say, 'Oh, fine, Meg, what a good idea. You go off to Edinburgh and forget all about me. Fine.' Is that what you thought I'd say?"

"I thought you'd understand."

"Oh yes, I do understand. Only too well. I was wrong about you, Meg. I thought you had some strength of character. I loved you."

His hands were holding hers; he was very close. For a heart-stopping moment Meg thought he was going to kiss her. If he did she would give up everything for him; she'd tell her parents she wasn't going to Scotland, her future was here with James. Every instinct told her to step forward into his embrace, but something held her back. Angrily he turned away.

"That's it then. Goodbye, Meg."

She stood still, watching him walk away along the cliff path, her eyes on his retreating figure until he turned the corner and was out of sight. Only then did she sink down onto the bench and let the tears come unchecked.

This is the last time I do this, she told herself fiercely. After this *no one* is ever going to tell me what to do with my life!

CHAPTER
NINE

Isobel's departure was hard for Meg, but she made sure that no one would suspect it. She threw herself into the farm, up early in the mornings and hard at work until late at night.

She was unusually sharp with Will when she found him playing with his puppy instead of getting on with his homework. "Will! Have I not told you to leave that puppy alone? He's supposed to be a working dog, not a pampered pet!"

"Sorry, Mother." Will got to his feet reluctantly. "I thought I'd go down to the village —"

"Oh no you won't! Haven't you got an essay to finish?"

"Well . . ."

"Away you go, then, and finish it. Then you can give me a hand out here."

Will went inside, seething. Work, work, work. Did his mother think of nothing else? He decided to have a quick word with Jeannie. There was something to do with the essay that he wasn't quite sure about and he felt in need of her advice. He pushed open the kitchen door and stuck his head round, hoping to find her there, but his heart sank when he saw only Ina, sitting with her feet up by the fire, reading a magazine.

He was going to go out again but Ina called him back.

"Master Will!"

He sighed. "Hello, Ina."

"Hello there." She got up and came towards him, smiling insolently. "Looking for your sweetheart, were you?"

"If you mean Jeannie, she's not my sweetheart!"

"Oh, really. Well, you do surprise me. And talking of sweethearts, I *am* surprised at your mother. At her age!"

"What do you mean?"

"Ooh, don't know if I should say . . ."

Will felt himself growing angry. He advanced on Ina. "You tell me!"

"All right then. I suppose you should know, seeing as you might be getting a new daddy."

"What? I don't believe you!"

"All right then, try asking your mother. Ask her what Dod Grant was saying to her in the parlour. Wasn't he just asking her to marry him? Romantic, don't you think?"

Will felt like laughing out loud. What a preposterous idea! She must be making it up.

Then he thought back. Dod Grant had certainly been around a lot lately, and all dressed up too. Most unlike him. And he and Meg had spent a lot of time alone in the parlour, and his mother had seemed very preoccupied afterwards. Maybe her funny mood wasn't due to Isobel's departure after all. And the clinching argument — he felt sure that Ina was perfectly capable of listening at doors. She'd probably heard the whole thing. He stared at her, dumbstruck.

Ina grinned. "I knew that would make you stop and think. Can't wait to spread the good news."

Will swallowed hard. "No, Ina, you mustn't."

"Well, what's it worth to you? Your mother's good name. You must care a fair bit."

"All right." He dug in his pockets and found nothing. "If you'll just wait a while."

"Till tomorrow. No longer."

"Fine." He sighed to himself. He'd have to ask his mother for an advance on his allowance. And in her odd mood she might be awkward about it. But Dod Grant! For heaven's sake! She'd be the laughing stock of the neighbourhood if that got out! It would have to get out sooner or later — but maybe she'd have second thoughts. Surely she would!

He turned and went out, cursing Ina under his breath. Then he stopped suddenly; Jeannie was coming across the yard, staggering under the weight of a sack of potatoes.

"Here, let me take those for you."

"I can manage." She made to go past him and he saw that her face was streaked with tears.

"What's the matter? I can see something is."

He stood in front of her, barring her way, and after a brief hesitation she put the sack down. "It's my mother. She's not well, and she has to work so hard. I'm fair worried about her."

"Have you been to see her?"

"How can I? I haven't time to get up there. It's too far to walk."

"I'll take you tomorrow if you like. It's your afternoon off, isn't it? We could take the trap."

"Could we?" Jeannie began to look hopeful. "But no, I couldn't ask that of you."

"It's no trouble. I'm sure my mother would agree if she knows the reason. I'll go and ask her now."

Before Jeannie could react, Will picked up the sack of potatoes and carried it into the kitchen. To his relief Ina was no longer there. He winked at Jeannie and went to find his mother, eventually coming across her in the rick yard. He explained what he wanted, and she agreed instantly.

"Of course you can take the trap. Poor Mrs Duncan! It's hard for her, trying to raise that big family single-handed. I'll send her a joint of pork, or maybe a chicken, and a couple of loaves with some fresh butter."

"Thanks, Ma." He stopped for a moment, then took a deep breath, "Oh, and by the way, could I possibly get an advance on my allowance? Just a bit of it?"

Meg turned and looked at him suspiciously. "An advance? May I ask why?"

"Oh, I —" He stared at the ground, hoping for inspiration. "It's my pal Ted's birthday."

"And you've nothing left from last month? Really, Will, I've always advised you to keep a bit by for things like that. I can't believe you've got through your money so quickly."

Will shuffled his feet. "Sorry."

103

Meg sighed. "All right, just this once. But I have no cash in the house at the moment. I've just paid the carter. I'll have to go to the bank tomorrow."

"Thanks." Will went back to the house, feeling anxious. Would that be soon enough for Ina?

He expected her to come after him the next day, but he saw nothing of her before he and Jeannie set off together in the trap, with a basket of groceries for her mother. It was a pleasant autumn day and Will was enjoying himself as they bowled along.

"So what do you usually do in your time off?" he asked.

"Not a lot. Sometimes I go into town, go to the library."

"Oh, come on! You can't be studying all the time, not even you! What else do you do?"

Jeannie laughed. "I like to look at the shops. And eat a sandwich in the gardens on Union Terrace. Feed the pigeons."

"That doesn't sound very exciting."

"Maybe not. But it's more exciting than being a skivvy."

Will said nothing. Jeannie went on, "But I tell myself it's only for now. When I've saved up enough I'll get to college."

"Do you really think you will?"

"Of course. It's the only thing that keeps me going. I just wish —"

"What?"

"Oh, that sometimes I had time for other things. Like going dancing."

"Do you like dancing?"

"I used to. I haven't been for ages."

"I'll take you." The words were out before Will could think twice; he felt amazed at his own boldness. He stole a glance at Jeannie and saw surprise on her face too.

"Do you really mean that?"

"'Course I do. Next weekend at the village hall. Will you come?"

Jeannie looked unsure. "Do you think it would be all right? Would the mistress not mind?"

"Why should she? She likes you."

"Well . . . all right then. Thank you. Oh and by the way?"

"Yes?"

"This is our house. If you don't stop you'll be past it."

Will pulled on the reins and directed the pony down the narrow track to a dilapidated-looking cottage. Looking around at the weedy yard and tumbledown outbuildings, he felt a sense of amazement that Jeannie could have such ambitious plans coming from a background such as this.

A group of poorly dressed children came out of the cottage and stared. "My brothers and sisters," Jeannie explained. She jumped down and ran over to them. "Don't you remember your big sister? I haven't been away that long!" Scooping up the smallest into her arms, she went inside, leaving Will outside in the yard, wondering what to do.

He had just decided to follow her indoors when a boy of about his own age came round a corner and stood eyeing him curiously. Will felt the need to introduce himself. He climbed down from the trap and walked over.

"Hello, I'm Will Fraser from Braeside. You must be Jeannie's brother."

"Aye, I'm Sandy." The boy looked him over, his expression guarded.

Will persevered. "Do you still live at home?"

"Aye, more's the pity. She" — he jerked his head in the direction of the cottage — "won't let me away. Wants me to get more schooling, but I've nae a mind for it."

"I know how you feel." Will sensed a soulmate. "My mother's the same. Is this your dog?"

He bent and stroked the black and white collie who bounded up to them. "Aye, that's Jess. She's just had a litter — want to see them?"

Will knew he had found a friend.

Inside the cottage, Mrs Duncan watched the two boys crossing the yard. "So that's the son of the house, is it? A fine young lad."

Jeannie, buttering bread at the table, nodded. "He and Sandy should get on well. Neither of them likes book learning."

Mrs Duncan sniffed. "It's all right for the likes of young Master Fraser. He has a grand farm coming to him one day. Things are different for our Sandy."

Jeannie said nothing; she knew it was pointless. She contented herself with doling out thick slices of bread and butter to her brothers and sisters. "Don't eat so fast — there's plenty more! And gingerbread for afters. Mind you eat all your bread first."

Her mother was still watching Will and Sandy. "Good of the lad to bring you over. Does he often take you out in the trap?"

"No, this is the first time. I told him you weren't well. Mistress Fraser sent a bottle of Dr Nicol's tonic, by the way, as well as the basket of food."

"Good of her. She's a generous woman at heart, for all they say she drives a hard bargain. It's not easy being a woman on her own."

"I know, Mother. You've both of you done well in your own way."

"And both of us wanting the best for our children. A good office job for Sandy there, and as for you —"

Jeannie said nothing. She wondered if her mother was about to relent; to admit that her daughter's future lay in going to college.

"You're doing well for yourself at Braehead."

"What? As a kitchen maid?"

"No. As the future lady of the house. Well done, my girl! If you play your cards right you've got that young lad just where you want him."

Jeannie felt her cheeks burning. "Mother! If you think that's what I'm doing —"

"And why not? It's what any lassie with a bit of sense would do!"

"But we're too young for anything like that, even if I was interested, which I'm not. And neither is he!"

"You think so?"

Jeannie said nothing. She remembered Will asking her to the dance, herself accepting. At the time she'd been thrilled, but now, after what her mother had just said, she wasn't so sure. Would people say she was trying to catch Will? Making up to him for what she could get out of it?

I can't go, she told herself fiercely. I'll tell him I've thought better of it. It would be a mistake.

"Oh, Will," Meg called to her son as he came across the yard after putting the pony in the stable. "I'm sorry, I didn't have time to go to the bank today."

"Oh." Will stood still, overcome by sudden panic. He'd promised Ina. What would she do when he reneged on his word?

"Don't look so stricken," his mother said. "It's not the end of the world."

"I know. But I'd promised — I mean, it's Ted's birthday."

"Well, you should have thought of that, shouldn't you, before you spent all your money. Let that be a lesson to you."

Will mumbled something. He turned and walked quickly across the yard, kicking at stones as he went. Everything was going wrong. Jeannie had been unaccountably distant on the way home, and when they'd got back she'd suddenly said she wouldn't be able to go to the dance after all. No attempt at an excuse or anything. And now the news that he wouldn't be able to pay off Ina; she was bound to be difficult about it.

In search of privacy, he climbed up into the hayloft and sat down on the floor. What was he going to do? His resentment increased. Who did Ina think she was, ordering him about like this? Did she think she could get money out of him for ever? Well, she was wrong. He couldn't give her any if he didn't have it, but why should he anyway?

She was probably making the whole thing up about Dod Grant, he decided, just to get money out of him. The whole idea was preposterous. Dod Grant never had a romantic notion in his head. As for Jeannie helping him with homework; well, let Ina go ahead and tell his mother about that. He didn't care. He knew that his mother had become fond of Jeannie, whereas she was constantly having to tell Ina off about her lazy slapdash ways. No, it was obvious that she would take Jeannie's side. So really he had nothing to fear from Ina, and he was going to tell her just that. Whistling a cheerful air, he climbed down from the loft.

He met Ina by the back door. She grinned at him expectantly. "Leaving it a bit late, weren't you? I was just thinking I'd like to have a good gossip with my pals."

"Well, go ahead then," Will said curtly. "Gossip all you like. No one will believe a word."

Ina stared. "You think so?"

"I know so. Because it's all lies, isn't it? Well, I'm not putting up with it any more. You can get lost."

With that he walked past her and into the house, hoping he looked a lot more confident than he felt.

Over the next few days he was sure he'd got away with it and called Ina's bluff. She gave him malevolent glances, but that was all. His mother presented him with the advance he'd requested but he made no attempt to give Ina anything. Instead he bought a present for Ted, even though his birthday was a good fortnight away. But buying it eased his conscience.

A telegram arrived from Isobel, telling of her safe arrival back in France. Meg was relieved; she knew the perils of a Channel crossing, and was always on edge until she knew her daughter had reached dry land.

"Though she's not exactly safe out there in a war zone," she told Ellen Nicol over tea a few days later.

"Surely the hospitals are secure though? Even the enemy will respect them."

"One hopes so. But Isobel told me that another hospital was bombed, even though it had big red crosses on the roof. They said it was a mistake, but even so."

"Oh dear. Let's hope it will all be over soon," Ellen said. She shook her head. "But how many times now have we said it will all be over by Christmas?"

"Too many. So we won't say it. More tea?"

Ellen accepted a cup. "Thanks. By the way . . ." She hesitated.

"What is it?" Meg looked anxiously at her friend. She had sensed there was something the matter; Ellen had appeared unusually restrained. "Dr Jim isn't worse, is he?"

"No, not at all. Back at work, even though he shouldn't be. And Donald is doing surprisingly well so far with his new business. We're all fine."

Meg put down the teapot. "But there is something wrong, isn't there? Better out with it."

"Well, it's rather difficult." Ellen fiddled with her teaspoon. "You see, it concerns you."

"Me?" Meg laughed. "I wouldn't worry about it, Ellen, people are always gossiping about me. I'm used to it. And as I'm not prepared to sit quietly at home doing my sewing and going to Guild meetings, then they'll keep on doing it. I'm surprised that you take any notice."

"Yes, but this is different. Oh, I don't know how to put it, and it's completely ridiculous but here goes. There's a rumour abroad that you're going to marry Dod Grant."

Meg went pale. She remembered her visit to the village shop that morning, the way the group of women at the counter had gone quiet when she'd walked in. The sly smiles from the men outside the chandlers, the quickly stifled sniggers from a couple of the younger farm workers. So that was it!

"Well, there's no truth in it," she said flatly.

Ellen sighed, clearly relieved. "I thought there couldn't be. The very idea!"

"He did ask me though."

"He did?" Ellen choked on her tea.

"Yes. He'd spoken about merging our two farms, and I was prepared to go along with that. I didn't realize that marriage was part of the deal. When he told me that it was I backed out of the whole thing."

"Good heavens! But how could the news have got out? I can scarcely imagine that Dod would want it known, given that you turned him down."

Meg frowned. "Nor can I. Unless he feels it might make me change my mind. In which case he's going to be disappointed."

"It's going to make life difficult for you, dear, whoever spread the news. People are bound to talk."

"Let them. Since when has that bothered me?"

But inwardly Meg was troubled. Normally she was impervious to gossip, but having her name linked with Dod's was hard to take. And why would anyone deliberately spread the rumour? It looked as though someone was deliberately out to damage her good name.

She said goodbye to Ellen, still preoccupied. Then the sound of her name called across the farmyard made her stop and turn. A messenger boy from the post office was hurrying towards her.

"Telegram from Miss Isobel, Mistress Fraser."

"Isobel?" All other thoughts were wiped from Meg's mind as she handed over some coppers to the boy and took the telegram from him. She realized that her hands were shaking.

She was suddenly conscious of the concerned glances from the men in the yard. Telegrams were always thought of as bad news. She couldn't open it there, not in front of them all. Slowly she walked back to the house, and only then, in the privacy of the parlour, did she sit down and open the envelope.

What she read made her head spin. She could hardly believe it. But the neatly printed words spelled it out inexorably:

DAVID MISSING PRESUMED KILLED. WHAT SHALL I DO? ISOBEL.

CHAPTER
TEN

As soon as Meg saw Mr Gillespie, the minister of the local church, driving his pony and trap up the track to the farm she knew that he must have come to commiserate with her.

She hurried into the house and called through to the kitchen, "Jeannie, the minister's on his way. Could you put the kettle on, please, and cut some gingerbread — he's very partial to a slice."

Quickly she pulled off her boots and rough sacking apron and put them behind the door, smoothing down her old work skirt as she pushed her feet into slippers. Fortunately she had known Mr Gillespie long enough to be sure that he would think nothing of her down-to-earth appearance. It was good of him to call and offer his support, but all the same she couldn't help wishing he hadn't come. She sighed. Now she faced the prospect of half an hour or so's chat about something she found extremely painful; far better, and more productive, to be out on the farm inspecting the newly dug drainage ditches. That way there would be no time for her mind to dwell fruitlessly on the agonizing details of what could have happened to David Falconer.

But Mr Gillespie saw none of this when he was shown into the front parlour by Jeannie. He found Meg standing by the fire with a ready smile for him.

"It's good to see you, Mr Gillespie. Come and warm yourself by the fire. The weather has turned very cold over the last twenty-four hours."

"Indeed it has, Mistress Fraser." The elderly minister accepted the invitation with alacrity, holding out his hands to the blaze that Meg had stirred up. "Winter's on its way and no mistake."

"I hope not quite yet," Meg demurred. "There's a lot to be done before then."

"So there is. And as if you haven't enough to think about, now there's this terrible news. I couldn't help hearing about your daughter's young man. What a great sadness for her, and you too."

"Yes, it's dreadful. I can still hardly believe it. But one mustn't give up hope. David has only been reported missing, not —"

She stopped, suddenly remembering that the minister and his wife had had similar news about their son-in-law, an infantry captain, only a year or so previously. They had been optimistic, but eventually their hopes had been dashed. She saw the lines of grief etched into the elderly man's face, and instinctively put out a hand. "I'm so sorry; this must bring back terrible memories for you and your family."

Mr Gillespie shook his head. "We're not the only ones to be affected. So many families have lost loved ones. And you yourself, your dear husband."

115

Meg looked away into the dancing flames. "Yes. It's hard. Please God it will all soon be over."

"Amen to that."

Jeannie came in with a tray of tea and gingerbread. Mr Gillespie had a few words with her, then when she had left he turned to Meg.

"That's the Duncan lassie, isn't it? How do you find her?"

"Very capable. She's not afraid of hard work, and she's an intelligent lass. I'm very pleased with her."

"A pity that circumstances prevented her from following her true vocation, though."

"What do you mean?" Meg paused in the act of pouring the tea and gave the minister a quizzical glance.

"Why, she wanted to go to college and train as a teacher. I was very disappointed when Jeannie's mother insisted on taking her away from the school and putting her to work. But of course the family needed the income."

"I hadn't realized that. Jeannie never said anything." Meg frowned as she handed over a cup of tea. "It doesn't surprise me, though. I'm sure she'd make an excellent teacher."

"Little prospect of her achieving it, I'm afraid."

"Mm." Meg stored the information away in her mind to be dealt with at a later date. She felt that she'd like to try to help Jeannie, but right at that moment her preoccupation with Isobel's plight was uppermost in her thoughts.

Mr Gillespie returned to that topic. "No further news then?"

"No. I don't know whether that's good or bad. But I'm very concerned for Isobel."

"Of course. At a time like this a girl needs her mother. I expect you'll be wanting to go out to her — or perhaps she'll be given compassionate leave? You might be able to meet in London?"

"Oh no, there's no question of that. I can't leave the farm and what good would it do, dashing down to see Isobel? It wouldn't help her or David."

There was a clatter as Mr Gillespie almost dropped his cup. He stared at Meg. "But surely —"

His face said it all. Immediately Meg realized she was once again being cast as the hard woman, the unfeeling mother. She felt the injustice of it deeply.

"Really, Mr Gillespie, if I thought I could do anything I would go at once. But if I turned up at the hospital I'd only be in the way, and I know myself at these times hard work is often the best antidote to worry. I've sent Isobel a telegram and I'll write as soon as I can. She's definitely in my thoughts and prayers."

"I see." The minister's tone was stiff, but Meg felt he was struggling to understand. There was a short silence then he said gruffly, "Perhaps you would like me to offer up a word of prayer for you both?"

Meg bent her head while the minister said a few words. Then he asked, "What about the young man's family? Are you in touch with them? You could perhaps be a comfort to each other?"

"No, I thought it best not to trouble them." Meg's tone was firm. "I've no wish to complicate things."

She resisted Mr Gillespie's attempts to make her change her mind and get in touch with David's father. She hadn't seen or heard from James Falconer for over twenty years. How could she possibly approach him now, under such harrowing circumstances? It wouldn't be right to intrude upon his grief.

Isobel lay on her hard camp bed in the staff quarters of the army hospital and stared up at the grey roof of her tent. She could hear the rain drumming down on the canvas, and from outside the shouts and curses of the medical orderlies as they struggled through the quagmire of mud. Her head throbbed and she closed her eyes, hoping for the sleep that wouldn't come.

Everyone was being so kind. The patients all sympathized; young Dr Falconer had been a favourite of theirs, and they all had a soft spot for Isobel. She remembered one soldier, a grizzled old amputee, grasping her hand as she straightened his sheets. "Don't give up hope, love," he'd whispered. "That young man of yours can look after himself. He'll be back, I'm sure of it."

Isobel had smiled down at him and squeezed his hand, grateful for his concern, but she hadn't been able to share his optimism. She'd seen too much of the casualties of war; she knew the damage that shells and bullets could cause. No, the chances were that David was one of the many who fell out in no-man's land and were never recovered. She simply had to get used to that fact.

"Asleep yet?" The whisper made her turn over and open her eyes as her tent mate, a shadowy figure in the gloom, came in from the cold evening.

Isobel struggled up onto one elbow. "No. I'm not really tired."

"Not tired? But you've been at it since six this morning, and the prospect of same again tomorrow. If you can't sleep you should ask them to give you something."

"I can't do that. They need all the supplies for the patients, and anyway, I don't want to be drugged into sleep. Suppose news came —"

She stopped, fighting back tears. "But it's not going to come, is it? We all know that. David's dead, and he's never going to come back. Never."

Her friend sat on the next low bed. "You know, it might be best if you make yourself believe that. You can't let yourself build up false hopes." She reached out a hand to Isobel's forehead. "Good grief, girl, you're on fire! You've got a temperature. Does Sister Marchmont know about this?"

"I'll be all right —"

"I'm not so sure. Perhaps I should go and get someone to take a look at you."

"No!" Isobel lay back. It was true, she really did feel dreadful, but she'd put it down to worry about David. Surely she couldn't be ill, on top of everything? She couldn't let herself be ill; she needed the distraction of her work. It was the only thing that kept her from dwelling on what might have happened to David. She didn't dare face the awful prospect of being alone with her thoughts.

"Well, we'll see how you are in the morning," her friend reluctantly conceded, and Isobel, too weary to argue, turned over and tried to get to sleep.

The next morning she reported for duty in a haze. Fortunately there'd been no new admissions during the night and it looked as though it would be a quiet day. She started on the daily round of temperatures, hoping there would be no emergencies. Just as she reached her third patient, she heard her name called.

"Miss Fraser?"

"Oh, Sister Marchmont." Isobel turned as the ward sister walked up to her, wondering why she was being called. "Are we expecting some new patients?"

"Not to my knowledge. I'd like a word with you as soon as you've finished your round."

"Very well, Sister."

Mechanically Isobel read the thermometer and entered the details on the man's chart, but inwardly her thoughts were racing. Had she done something wrong? Some lapse in concentration the previous day that was about to catch up with her? Maybe it was that spilt Jeyes Fluid — she'd wiped it up quickly and flushed the area with water, but the smell was bound to linger and she might have earned herself a reprimand for being careless with scarce resources.

"Don't you fret, Nurse," her patient said, grinning up at her. "We'll put in a good word for you if you need it. Don't let her boss you about."

120

Isobel returned his smile, and somehow made herself concentrate on her job as she finished off the routine task. If only her head didn't feel so fuzzy! Normally she was confident in her own abilities, but in this state she couldn't be sure she'd done everything right.

She walked up to the makeshift table at the end of the tented ward where Sister Marchmont sat.

"Ah, Miss Fraser." The sister's expression was kind, but her gaze was shrewdly assessing. "How are you feeling today?"

"I —" Taken off guard, Isobel floundered. "I'm perfectly well, thank you, Sister."

"Permit me to disagree. I think you are anything but well, Miss Fraser, and that is why I am giving you a week's leave."

"A week!" Isobel gasped. "But I really don't need it, and besides, who will cover for me?"

"Cover is not a problem. We have a batch of new recruits coming out tomorrow. Not a patch on you, of course, but they can be licked into shape. And I do think you need it, Miss Fraser. Have you looked at yourself recently? Those dark circles under your eyes. And you've been losing weight — I can tell that from your uniform."

She held up a hand imperiously as Isobel tried to speak. "You are no use to us if you are not one hundred per cent fit. I want you to go away and get yourself well. I don't suppose there's time for you to get yourself all the way up to Scotland at this short notice, and with transport the way it is I'm not convinced it would be wise. I believe you have relatives in the south of England? I'm sure they'd be happy to see you."

"I suppose so." Isobel made one last plea. "But I've not long been home on leave. Surely I can't be spared again so soon?"

Sister Marchmont raised an eyebrow. "Are you questioning my decision, Miss Fraser?"

"No, of course not, but —"

"No buts. You have had a harrowing time lately; you need to get over it. God knows it won't be easy for you." She paused, her eyes suddenly far away, and Isobel remembered rumours that Sister Marchmont had once had a sweetheart in the Royal Flying Corps, a pilot who had been shot down over enemy lines. She wondered whether to say anything, but before she could Sister Marchmont was once again her brusque self. "Your rail warrant will be here this afternoon. Now I suggest you go and make up the dressing trolley."

"Yes, Sister. And . . . thank you."

Isobel walked away with mixed feelings. To be honest she didn't really want to leave her work, but then a week away would give her time to get over her cold or whatever it was that was making her feel so unwell. She wondered about mentioning it to the sister, but decided against it. No point in complicating things; a few days spent with her godmother in Kent would soon see her right. And if she got back to find David safe and well, then everything would be perfect, wouldn't it?

If only she could convince herself.

CHAPTER
ELEVEN

"I'm sorry, Annie, but it's not good news." Dr Jim frowned as he sat down in the Duncans' cramped kitchen. Washing hung around them in damp folds, and the atmosphere was clammy and chill despite the fire.

"What do you mean, Doctor? Surely you can give me a dose of your tonic and I'll be right as rain. It's always worked for me in the past."

"Oh, Annie!" Dr Jim had to smile. "Thank you for your ringing endorsement of my medicines but, no, I'm afraid your problem is something that tonic won't fix this time. I'm afraid, my dear, it looks like a stay in hospital, perhaps even an operation."

"An operation!" Mrs Duncan's hand flew to her mouth. "But I can't afford anything like that!"

"Don't worry about it, Annie, it won't cost you anything, I'll see to that."

"It's not just that, Doctor." Mrs Duncan got up and began to pace around distractedly, automatically feeling at the hanging washing to see if it was drying. "No — my work, the washing. I need the money. What would become of the family?"

"I'm sure your regular customers would come back to you —" Dr Jim began, but he was interrupted.

123

"Maybe they would, but who's to say? They might find someone they liked better. And anyway, how long would I be away?"

"A couple of weeks, perhaps, but then you'd have to take things easy for a while after."

"I can't do that!" Mrs Duncan's face was distraught. "We owe money at the shop as it is. No, I'll just have to keep on going. I'll be all right, you'll see."

Dr Jim shook his head. "No, Annie, you won't be all right. If you keep on like this it's only a matter of time before you land yourself in hospital for a good deal longer than two weeks. I don't want to frighten you, lass, but you have to believe me."

Mrs Duncan sank down into a seat. "But I can't —"

"Let's think about it. How old is young Sarah?"

"She's eleven."

"Well, with a bit of help from your neighbour down the road she could keep house here and look after the younger two. All three of them are at school all day, aren't they? And there's your lad Sandy — what's he up to these days?"

"He's at school." Mrs Duncan spoke flatly, all the spirit knocked out of her. She was just skin and bone, Dr Jim noted sadly, worn out by years of hard work and little money.

"Sandy might like to leave school and get work," the doctor suggested. He'd heard that Sandy was a very unwilling scholar, and he couldn't help thinking the boy would jump at this chance to leave. But to his dismay Mrs Duncan shook her head.

124

"No, the lad needs his chance. He's got to carry on with his schooling."

Nothing Dr Jim could say would convince her, either to let Sandy leave the school or to agree to go into hospital. He left with a heavy heart, insisting only that she get in touch with him straight away if she should feel any worse, or if she changed her mind.

Out in the yard he found Sandy with Will Fraser. They greeted him cheerfully.

"How's my mother, Dr Nicol?" Sandy asked. "Have you brought another bottle of that tonic? I don't know what she'd do without the stuff." Then he saw the doctor's troubled expression, and he stiffened. "There's something wrong, isn't there?"

Will moved away. "I'll just get a load of firewood in for Mrs Duncan," he said tactfully. "You have a chat with the doctor, Sandy."

Quickly Dr Jim explained the situation. Sandy reacted just as he would have expected. "She must go into hospital," he said. "We'll manage."

"How?"

"I'll leave school. She can't stop me now. The dear knows, I'm wasting my time there. I want to do farm work."

"Have you any thoughts on where you'd go?"

"Aye, I have. Will was only just saying that they'll be needing a new hand at Braeside come term day. Maybe they'd take me early. That would be just perfect, wouldn't it?"

"It certainly would." Dr Jim felt distinctly hopeful. "And your sister's already there. It would be excellent if

125

you were both together. Too good to be true. But would your mother agree?"

"I'll convince her." Sandy sounded definite. "To be honest, I think she's worried about her health. If I'm earning as well as Jeannie there's nothing to stop her going in to the hospital for as long as it takes. It'll be all right, you'll see."

"Good lad." Dr Jim clapped Sandy on the shoulder. "I'll leave it with you. Let me know how you get on. But the sooner we get that mother of yours into hospital the happier I'll be. She can't go on the way she is."

He climbed into his pony trap and drove off, leaving Sandy staring after him. Will came out of the house, looking concerned. "Sandy, your mother's crying. I think you should go to her. Is there anything I can do?"

"Maybe there is. Do you think you could persuade your ma to give me a job?"

Sandy explained briefly, and Will's face broke into a grin. "You bet I could! That would be great! She was only saying the other day that so many of the best lads have gone off to join the army, she didn't know what she was going to do. She'd be glad to have you. I'll put in a good word for you, explain the situation. Now you'd better go in and help your mother."

"I'll do that. Thanks. You're a good friend."

Sandy turned and hurried inside. Thoughtfully Will got on his bike and started to pedal home. His thoughts were mixed. It would be wonderful to have Sandy at Braehead — they shared a passion for farming and the land, and he knew it would help Sandy's mother. But how would Jeannie take the prospect of her brother

126

joining her at Braehead? She'd been very distant lately, avoiding his company and hardly exchanging a word when they did meet. Had Ina been making trouble? he wondered. He knew she was spiteful enough to make life very awkward for Jeannie. If Sandy got involved, things could turn nasty. Ina was keeping company with the farm's third horseman, a young fellow from Speyside; she might stir up trouble between him and the newcomer. Sandy might find a very awkward situation awaiting him.

Isobel stepped back from the shiny front door and looked up and down the suburban street. This couldn't be happening! She'd arrived at her godmother's house, footsore and weary, with a grinding headache, longing to sit down and be fussed over. But several minutes of knocking at the door had brought no response.

A surge of panic rose inside her, but she forced it down and tried to think logically. It was late afternoon, and she hadn't been able to send word ahead of her impending arrival. They might just be out; they could be back any minute.

But meanwhile she felt dreadful. She was hungry and thirsty, and worse, she felt cold and shivery despite her thick uniform coat. Not for the first time she questioned the wisdom of accepting the week's leave; she might have been better off staying in the hospital where at least she could have been looked after.

Still, here she was, and she couldn't just stand on the doorstep indefinitely. Heaving up her bag, she walked to the house next door and knocked.

It was opened by a tall cheerless woman who fixed her with a haughty stare. "Yes?"

Isobel summoned up a smile. "I wonder if you could tell me when the people next door will be back? There doesn't seem to be anyone in at the moment."

"There won't be. The family are all away to a wedding up north somewhere." The woman's manner conveyed that "up north" was beyond the reach of civilization.

"Oh, I see." Isobel managed to hide her plummeting sense of despair. She made a last attempt. "Is the housekeeper likely to be in?"

"Oh no. She's been given a holiday. The house is all shut up."

Isobel hesitated a moment, wondering if an invitation to come in would be forthcoming. Surely the woman could see that she'd travelled a long way and was desperately tired. But as she stood there, the door was implacably closed against her.

She turned away, her worst fears realized. There was only one option left for her now, she knew that, and it wasn't one she relished. She was going to have to make an approach to David's family.

She bit her lip. She hadn't mentioned this to her mother, but she was very uneasy at the way David's father had reacted to the news of his son's engagement. David hadn't said much to her about it, but Isobel knew he hadn't had the response he'd hoped for.

"It'll be all right, darling," he'd assured her. "It was a bit of a shock for poor old Pa, but he can't help but love you when he meets you."

128

Now Isobel questioned David's breezy self-assurance. Maybe David's father didn't think she was good enough for his precious only son. Perhaps he had someone else in mind. And she remembered what her mother had said about that old romance she'd had with David's father long ago; perhaps they had parted with bitterness. It could well be that Isobel Fraser was the last person James Falconer might want as a bride for his son.

But, she reminded herself, trying to be optimistic, Mr Falconer doesn't know I'm her daughter; he knew her as Meg Lacey. He won't make the connection. At least, I don't think he will. Doubt flooded through her — was it really a good idea to turn up where she might not be at all welcome? But she really had no choice.

She took out her diary from her pocket and scanned the scribbled address inside the front cover. Well, Mr Falconer, she thought, I hope you're in a good mood, because you're about to have an unexpected guest for supper.

"Cab, miss?" A line of horse-drawn cabs waited a little distance away. Isobel fingered the coins in her pocket; there should be enough. She could have walked but in her present weary state and with evening coming on it was good to be driven. She felt like a gambler making a last desperate throw; if this failed she didn't know what she would do, but she'd think about that when the time came. She gave the driver the address, and settled back in her seat.

It felt like only a few seconds when the vehicle came to a halt, and she realized she must have dozed off. The cabbie was holding the door for her.

"Here you are, miss."

Isobel looked out of the window and swallowed hard. They had stopped outside a pair of ornate iron gates. Beyond them was a large gracious house fronted by neat lawns. She took a deep breath.

Standing outside the cab, she felt strangely light-headed. It had been a long time since she'd eaten, she thought suddenly, as she paid the cabbie and made some answer to his parting comments. Then she picked up her bag and scrunched over the gravel to the front door, going over in her mind what she was going to say. She felt very much at a loss, and it was an unpleasant feeling.

She rang the bell, hearing it sound somewhere deep inside the house. It opened promptly and a neatly dressed maid greeted her. "Good evening, miss. Can I help you?"

"Good evening. I've come to see Mr Falconer. Is he at home?"

The maid looked doubtful. "Is Mr Falconer expecting you?"

Isobel felt a surge of panic. Was she about to be summarily turned away yet again? She couldn't let it happen. "No, he isn't, but I would very much like to speak to him. My name is Isobel Fraser, and I've come all the way from France. It's very important that I see Mr Falconer."

Another wave of light-headedness washed over her, and she put out a hand to the door frame for support. The maid gave her a concerned look. "Come in, Miss Fraser. You can sit down in the drawing-room. I'll see if Mr Falconer can see you."

Isobel followed her inside, scarcely noticing her surroundings. She sank into a chair in the well-appointed drawing-room and closed her eyes. It was tempting to give way to weariness and let herself simply fall asleep, but she knew she couldn't afford that luxury. It was imperative that she made a good impression on this man, who might, in happier circumstances, have become her father-in-law. Surely he would want to help her, for David's sake, if nothing else.

All the same she felt herself drifting away, until suddenly a voice rang in her ears and she was instantly wide awake. She hurried to her feet and turned to face the tall man who had just entered the room.

"Miss Fraser?" He sounded uncertain. "I'm James Falconer. What can I do for you?"

Isobel stared at him, her heart pounding. Yes, this was unmistakably David's father; she would have known him anywhere, even if she hadn't seen that photo in her mother's room.. He was so like his son. The dark hair was flecked with grey, and the lines round his eyes and mouth were deeper, but his figure was still upright and athletic. He wore a black armband, Isobel noted with a stab of compassion. Then as she watched, his expression gradually changed from one of polite interest to something close to amazement.

He must recognize me, she thought with a surge of relief. David must have sent him a photo. It's going to be all right!

His lips moved, but it was almost as if he were speaking to himself. Isobel, straining her ears, thought she heard the whispered words, "But it can't be! Meg — after all this time, but no —"

Isobel took a step forward. The words came tumbling out, faster than she would have liked, making her almost incoherent. "Mr Falconer, I'm — I mean, I was — David's fiancée — Meg's daughter — I'm over on leave, but I've nowhere to go —"

She stopped. The floor lurched under her feet. The room seemed to be slowly revolving. She heard James's voice from a far distance, calling her name — or was it her mother's? She tried to say something then everything went black.

CHAPTER
TWELVE

"Good morning, young Master Fraser! That's a fine collie pup you've got there!"

Will turned as he heard his name called across the farmyard. He grinned as he recognized the stocky figure of Dr Jim Nicol coming towards him. "Morning, Doctor! Yes, he's not bad, is he? Ma gave me the choice of the litter. Are you bringing us more of Mrs Nicol's jam?"

Dr Jim smiled back. "No such luck, I'm afraid. I'll pop in for a word with your mother — I was hoping to be in time for a spot of tea — but I was really wanting to see the young Duncans. Do you know where they'll be?"

"I just left Sandy in the stables, cleaning up some harness," Will told him. "He's settled in fine here. Jeannie will be in the house somewhere. It'll be about their mother, I suppose," he added, a touch anxiously. "I hope she's all right."

"Aye, she's as well as can be expected. But she'll be a lot better after tomorrow; she's due to have her operation. I thought the two of them should know."

"Oh, of course. If you'd like to go along in you should find Jeannie. I'll get Sandy for you."

Will hurried off to find his friend.

Later he met Sandy coming back to the stables, his face set. He managed a grin when he saw Will, but he was clearly concerned. Will tried to be reassuring.

"She'll be all right, chum, she's in good hands. She'll be right as rain in no time."

"I know," Sandy responded, looking away. "But you can't help worrying. Doc Nicol says we can't visit her until the day after — suppose she's asking for us?"

"They'll explain. And anyway, she'll probably be feeling pretty groggy. I remember after I had a couple of teeth out, I felt ghastly —" Will paused, wondering if he'd said the right thing. Hastily he changed the subject. "How's Jeannie taking it?"

A mistake. Sandy looked worried. "Badly. She's blaming herself for Mum taking ill; saying she upset her by arguing about wanting to stay on at school, all that stuff. I know it's rubbish. Dr Nicol says Mum's problem is from too much hauling heavy weights about over the years, but Jeannie thinks she should have done more to help."

"I'm sure she did all she could," Will said.

"I told her that, but she wasn't havin' any of it. Once our Jeannie gets an idea into her head it's hard to get it out again."

"I'll see what I can do." Will spoke with more conviction than he felt, but he thought he should at least try to comfort Jeannie. He didn't like the thought of her in distress.

He went into the house to look for her, but she wasn't there. His mother was out too; through the window he caught sight of her striding off down to the rick yard, a two-pronged fork in her hand. He smiled at the sight. Mother was such a character, careless of what people thought. She was as hard a worker as any of the farmhands.

Suddenly remembering what Sandy had said, he frowned. Might his own mother finish up in a similar situation to poor Mrs Duncan? Perhaps he should have a word with her about leaving the heavy work for the men. Meanwhile he had to find Jeannie; he went outside in search of her.

He found her in the hen run, scattering a basket of corn for the fowls. She turned away as he approached, and he thought he saw the glint of tears on her cheek. He pretended he hadn't noticed.

"Hello, how's things?"

She didn't answer at first. Will waited until she'd emptied her basket of grain, then she said quietly, "They've been better. I suppose Sandy's told you about Mum?"

"That she's having her operation tomorrow? Yes, he has."

"I should be with her!" Jeannie said fiercely. "She'll be wanting me, I know she will. She'll be frightened —"

"Look." Will took a step forward. "She'll be all right. She's in good hands, and once it's all over she'll be fine."

"I wish I could believe that." Jeannie dropped the basket and put her hands over her face, clearly very distressed. It was too much for Will. He reached out and put his arms round her, stroking her hair.

"Don't worry, Jeannie. Please don't upset yourself . . ."

He thought she might push him away, but she didn't; she just stood there, sobbing quietly into his shoulder. Then, suddenly, they heard a harsh cackle of laughter. Guiltily they jumped apart. Ina stood a little way off, hands on hips, surveying them with a sarcastic grin.

"Oh, well done, Miss Clever Clogs, I can see your game! Fancy yourself as the mistress here, do you?"

Jeannie went scarlet. Will opened his mouth, then shut it again. He was so angry he couldn't trust himself to speak. But he had to do something; he couldn't let Ina sneer at them like this.

As he hesitated another figure came into view. It was Sandy. He took one look at the situation and clearly summed up what was going on. He strode over to Ina.

"Haven't you got work to do?"

"Maybe I have. But what about that sister of yours? Looks like her work is getting her claws into the son of the house. She's a clever hussy —"

"Don't you dare say that about my sister!" Sandy bit out. "Get yourself back to your kitchen and keep your nose out of other folks' business. Or I'll be paying a bit more attention to yours, and see how you like that!"

He stared at Ina. Muttering something under her breath, she turned on her heel and flounced away. There was silence for a few moments, then Sandy turned to his sister. "Are you all right?"

Jeannie took a long slow breath. "Yes, thanks." She bent and picked up the basket then took her brother's arm. Together they walked towards the house, leaving Will staring after them, feeling totally inadequate. Why

136

couldn't he have faced up to Ina? Why did it have to be Sandy who'd seen her off? Jeannie would think he was a useless schoolboy, completely lacking any sort of moral authority.

And, he thought bitterly, as he walked slowly across the yard, maybe she's right.

Meg saw Dod Grant before he saw her. As she came round the corner of the stable into the rick yard, wheeling a barrow of turnips, she caught sight of him inspecting a few stalks of corn he'd pulled out from one of the stacks.

"Does it meet with your approval, Mr Grant?"

At the sound of her call, he started with alarm and dropped the stalks. Meg repressed a smile.

"It's a good harvest, mistress," he answered stiffly, "but I wonder if you'll have the same next year."

Meg looked at him. There was something in his tone that made her feel uneasy. "Why, I hope we shall, weather permitting. Farming is always a gamble, I suppose, but hard work reduces the risk."

"Aye, that it does."

He had obviously come on some errand. Meg parked the barrow by a wall. "You'll take a cup of tea, Mr Grant?"

"Thanks, mistress, I will."

She led the way to the farmhouse, making small talk, but inwardly her mind was racing. Dod had not visited the farm since she'd rejected his unwelcome proposals. Surely he wasn't planning to have another try? Unlikely, she thought, because he wasn't dressed in his

137

best as he had been on that occasion; he was wearing patched trousers and a threadbare jacket that had seen better days. No, this must be some more mundane matter, thank goodness.

She took him into the parlour, calling to Jeannie on the way through to bring a pot of tea and some shortbread. As they waited she tried a few probing questions, but it was only when the tea was poured and the polite chat exhausted that Dod at last got to the point.

"I was thinking about that culvert, ye know the one?"

"Of course. You're thinking it's time we cleaned it out? A good idea, because we're dependent on it here at Braehead for our water supply. When did you have in mind?"

"I didn't. I'm not minded to help maintain the thing. Why should I? It's no use to me."

"Indeed not. The benefit's all ours. But —" Meg stopped as a ghastly realization hit her. "You don't mean —"

"Aye, I do. I want rid of it. That culvert passes through my land, and never a penny have I had for my trouble."

"But Mr Grant, that's not true! Alistair paid you a very fair sum for your inconvenience when they were laying it, and since then — well, it's completely underground. You'd never know it was there."

"Ah, but I do know it's there, and what happens if it blocks? I've been noticing a boggy area down by the larches, and I don't like the look of it."

138

"Well, I'll be happy to come and attend to it," Meg began, but even as she spoke she knew it was hopeless. Dod had it in his power to cut off the bulk of the water supply to Braeside, and he fully intended to do it.

Later she wondered how she'd managed to keep her temper, but keep it she did, even though it was a very tight-lipped interview, and her tea and shortbread went untasted. But she could let her feelings out later when Ellen dropped round.

"I could have poured the tea over his head! To see him sitting there, saying how sorry he was but he'd made his decision — oh!"

"You're sure he really has made the decision?" Ellen asked, horrified. "Nothing could change his mind?"

"Well, I suspect that if I were to agree to become Mrs Grant things might be different," Meg said grimly. "He wouldn't want to take over an unviable farm, and that's what Braehead will be if he blocks off that culvert. I can't help feeling he's doing this to teach me a lesson; show me the error of my ways in not accepting him."

Ellen shuddered. "No, you did the right thing there! But, as for the water supply, surely you managed before you had the culvert?"

"Yes, but the farm was much smaller then. We have two wells on the property but they couldn't cope with our needs now. Alistair negotiated with Dod years ago to get the extra water so that the farm could expand."

"So there must be some legal agreement, or at least something in writing?"

Meg shook her head with a sigh. "No, there isn't. Alistair always took people on trust; a word and a handshake were enough for him. I did say to him at the time that he should go through a solicitor, but he said no, it was a gentleman's agreement."

"Dod Grant — some gentleman!" Ellen commented. "But Meg, this is a disaster. What on earth are you going to do?"

"Well, I'm not going to give up without a fight," Meg said with determination. "I need to see if we can deepen the wells we have, and I'll get a dowser in to see if we can find any new ones. I managed to persuade Dod to give us six months before the water supply gets cut off, so that gives us time to look for alternatives."

"Have you told anyone else?" Ellen asked.

"No. And I particularly don't want Will to hear about it — he'd be worried sick. I can't imagine Dod would want to spread it about either — he must realize that people would think badly of him."

"I won't mention it to Jim," Ellen promised. "As much for Dod Grant's sake as anything else. Jim would be furious; I wouldn't put it past him to go up there and give him a piece of his mind."

"I wouldn't like to be on the receiving end of that!" Meg managed to laugh. "And now, let's change the subject and talk about something more cheerful. I hear your Donald's doing well with his motor business."

She steered the conversation onto less worrying topics, but all the same she couldn't stop thinking about the very real threat to the future of the farm. It was as much as she could do to sit and chat to Ellen, when really she wanted to start work straight away on looking for alternative sources of water. Then they could show Dod Grant what they thought of him.

"Give my love to Jim," she said, as she went outside to see Ellen off. "And don't worry — we'll get through this." Then she stopped. Sandy Duncan was digging the garden not far from the open parlour window. Meg remembered she'd asked him to turn over a patch where she wanted to put fruit bushes. Could he have heard their conversation? She looked pointedly at him, but he just grinned and waved.

She turned away. No, she was imagining things. He'd been coming and going all afternoon; he wouldn't have heard anything. She had to believe it.

CHAPTER
THIRTEEN

"How is she, Doctor?" James Falconer strode to the foot of the stairs, trying to conceal his impatience as the doctor came down from examining Isobel.

"Have you a moment, Mr Falconer?" The doctor looked grave. "I'd appreciate a word."

"Of course. My study's over here." James led the way through a set of double doors into a book-lined room. "Have a seat. Can I get you a drink? Tea? Coffee? Or something stronger? A whisky perhaps?"

"A whisky would be very welcome. It's a cold day."

James went over to a drinks cupboard and poured a generous whisky. He was surprised to find his fingers were unsteady and some of the drink slopped on the carpet as he carried it over, but it seemed to pass unnoticed. He poured another for himself and took a mouthful, hoping it would soothe his nerves.

"Well, Doctor?"

"Very good whisky, Mr Falconer, a first-rate malt. Can't say I've tasted a better —"

"I'm not talking about the whisky, man. I mean how is Miss Fraser, your patient? I'm very concerned about her."

The doctor put down his glass. "So you should be, sir. She's not at all well. A combination of hard conditions over in France, inadequate food, long hours, and —"

"And?"

"Well, I fear there is an infection there. Maybe something she picked up in the army hospital, or maybe, though I hope not, she may have contracted the influenza."

James said nothing but his fingers tightened around his glass. He'd heard about the flu, this new illness that was sweeping across Europe. Some said it might even cost as many lives as the last four years of war. The thought of Isobel — Meg's daughter — falling victim to it was more than he could bear.

The doctor was speaking again; he forced himself to listen. "I strongly advise that you get her moved to the fever hospital as soon as possible. There is risk of the infection being passed on —"

"No!" James shot to his feet. "No," he said again, calming himself with an effort. "There can be no question of moving her. She must stay here. I'll engage a nurse."

"But, sir, you must consider your own safety. This can be a dangerous illness. In many cases it has proved fatal as you must know."

"I know that very well. But this young lady is the daughter of" — he paused for a moment — "of an old friend. I see it as my duty to do the best I can for her."

The doctor looked up at him, then spread his hands in a gesture of acquiescence. "Very well, if that is what you wish. I can recommend a nurse for you, and I will have the necessary medicines sent round. But I must warn you to be prepared for the worst. The next few days will be touch and go." He drained his glass and stood up. "The nurse will come straight away. I'll come back myself tomorrow."

"Thank you." James shook his hand and saw him to the front door. Then, left alone, he drained his whisky and sank back into his chair, eyes closed, his mind a chaos of emotion. So much had happened, it was almost more than he could cope with. First the loss of his son, now this! The news that David was missing presumed killed had been a crushing blow and he was only just beginning to come to terms with it. Then only a couple of hours ago Isobel, David's fiancée, had so unexpectedly entered his life, bringing the incredible knowledge that she was Meg Lacey's daughter! And now it seemed that Isobel too might be snatched away — James groaned as he imagined the heartache that would bring to Meg.

He sat up abruptly, filled with determination. Well, it was too late for David, but he was going to move heaven and earth to help Isobel. Nothing would be too much trouble or expense, she would have the very best of everything to help her fight this illness.

Then a new thought struck him. He'd have to write to her parents, let them know what was happening. What was her surname — Fraser? So Meg Lacey was Meg Fraser now. She had a husband in Scotland — Isobel's father. Maybe there were other children.

Whereas he had never remarried. His first wife, David's mother, had died when their son was just a baby, long before James had first met Meg. There'd been no one after Meg in his life; no one had measured up to her.

He frowned. It seemed that Meg had forgotten him so completely, had forged a new life for herself far away in the north of Scotland. She hadn't made any attempt to get in touch, and he had stayed aloof too — his pride had demanded it. Now, suddenly, he had to re-enter her life, bringing terrible news.

How would he find her address? Perhaps Isobel would have something — a notebook or something of the sort. He'd have to go and look. Or maybe she'd be awake and could tell him. He got to his feet and went upstairs.

He tapped gently on Isobel's door and went in. She was asleep, her face flushed and her hair spread out over the pillow. His heart thumped; even in her feverish state she had such a look of her mother. He sat down by the bed and took her hand in his. "Isobel?"

Her eyes flickered open and she stared at him. "Who —"

"Remember me? I'm" — he hesitated — "I'm David's father."

"Oh." She turned her head, and he saw her bite down on her lower lip. "I remember now. I turned up on your doorstep and flaked out. I must be causing you so much trouble. I'm sorry."

"Don't be. I'm glad to help. We must get you well again."

She turned back to him. "I don't want to be a nuisance."

"You're not, don't think it." He smiled and squeezed her hand. "You must have nursed so many soldiers in your time in France; now it's your turn to be looked after. How do you feel?"

She grimaced. "Awful."

"Oh dear. Well, we've got to get you right again. Some medicine's on its way, and there'll be a nurse coming to look after you." He paused. There were so many questions he wanted to ask her, so many gaps he wanted to fill, but he knew it would have to wait. There was just one piece of information he needed.

"Isobel, I'll leave you in peace for a while, but there's just one thing first. I want to write to your mother to let her know you're here, and I don't have the address. Could you tell me, please?"

"Oh, yes. That's — that's very kind of you." She told him the address and he noted it down.

"Thanks. Now you get some sleep."

Downstairs he sat at his desk, a blank sheet of paper in front of him, feeling unusually at a loss. What on earth was he going to say? How exactly did you frame a letter to a woman you had once loved — whom you *still* loved if you were honest with yourself — but who had effortlessly shut you out of her life?

He stared at the paper, wondering if Isobel knew of the connection. But it seemed unlikely that Meg would have volunteered anything to her daughter. It was even more unlikely that she'd spoken of him to her husband. So this letter would have to be very circumspect, giving them the news about Isobel's condition and no more than that. It would have to be couched in terms that were scrupulously formal; there could be no suggestion of any lingering affection.

A new thought occurred to him. If Isobel's illness continued to cause concern, or — God forbid — got any worse, Meg would want to come down to be with her. In fact, he really should invite her straight away. So maybe after over twenty years he was going to meet Meg again, and perhaps, for the first time, her husband. Not a prospect he looked forward to, but it had to be faced.

He took up his pen and began to write. It was difficult at first, but as he went on his pent-up thoughts flowed onto the page, almost more quickly than he could get them down. Eventually there were six closely written sheets to be folded into an envelope. Now he faced an anxious wait for Meg's reply; let it be soon, for Isobel's sake, he thought wearily.

Meg lay in bed unable to sleep. Far in the distance an owl hooted, answered by another one close to the house. Meg usually found the sound oddly comforting, but in her present frame of mind she couldn't help reflecting that the owl was traditionally a bird of ill omen. She shivered and pulled the blankets closer round her shoulders.

It had not been a good day. She'd been to see the solicitor in town to find out if anything could be done to safeguard the water supply, but the answer had been negative. In the absence of any written agreement it seemed that Dod Grant was perfectly within his rights to block up the culvert. The solicitor even went so far as to express his astonishment that the matter had not been put on a proper legal footing from the outset. What made it harder to bear was that privately Meg agreed with him. Alistair had been far too trusting. A decent, honourable man himself, he had made the mistake of thinking that everyone else measured up to his own high standards.

Well, Meg thought resignedly, there's nothing we can do about it now. We must look at the alternatives. Maybe she could offer to pay Dod something. An annual sum, perhaps, in return for the water supply across his land. He was well known for his grasping ways, so maybe that approach would be successful. He'd probably demand a high price though, and the farm budget was already overstretched.

I could always sell my ruby necklace, Meg thought. She didn't want to, because it had been handed down in Alistair's family for generations, and she had hoped to pass it on in due course to Will's bride, but if it saved the farm then surely the sacrifice would be worth it? But it shouldn't have come to this! She sat up and punched her pillow, trying to make it more comfortable.

Her mind turned to Isobel. Nothing had been heard from her for some time, and Meg was worried about how her daughter was coping with the loss of her fiancé. Of course communications were difficult in wartime and possibly Isobel had had good news; she certainly hoped so. She decided she would definitely write tomorrow, or maybe even send a telegram. It would at least do the girl good to know that her family and friends were thinking about her.

The strident noise of a cock crowing reminded Meg that dawn was on its way and she would soon have to be up. Another day of hard work after a sleepless night would surely take its toll. Sometimes it was very wearying having no one to confide in, no one to share her deepest concerns. She closed her eyes and tried to snatch a brief respite before the cares of the day crowded in on her.

It seemed only moments later that the ear-splitting din of the old brass alarm clock on the bedside table woke her from troubled dreams. Yawning, she got up, dressed in a daze and made her way down the stairs to the kitchen. There she found Jeannie Duncan coaxing the fire into life.

"Morning, Jeannie. Ina not down yet?"

"Mornin', ma'am. Er . . . she's on her way." Jeannie blew on the dull embers, keeping her back turned to Meg. She knew that Ina was still in bed, demanding that Jeannie take her a cup of tea or else she'd tell Mrs Fraser what she'd witnessed between Jeannie and Will. Jeannie wasn't sure if Ina would carry out her threat, but she didn't dare take the chance. With their mother in hospital it fell on herself and Sandy to earn the money to support the family, so she couldn't do anything that might risk dismissal. Jeannie knew that Mrs Fraser was a fair woman, but it was common knowledge that she had great ambitions for her only son, and an entanglement with a serving maid would not be looked upon with favour.

Fortunately for Jeannie, Meg went out to speak to the farm's foreman, leaving her alone in the kitchen. With the fire burning brightly, she put the kettle on to boil and set about making a pot of tea. While it was brewing she ladled oatmeal into a huge old pot, added water and put it on the range to make the porridge for the men's breakfast. That done, she poured a cup of tea and, looking round to make sure no one saw her, hurried up the stairs to Ina.

"About time! What kept you? Was your heartthrob, Master Will, down in the kitchen?"

Jeannie said nothing; just deposited the cup on the kist beside Ina's bed.

"How about a slice of toast to go with it?"

That was too much; Jeannie saw red. "You're lucky you got a cup of tea! I had to wait for the mistress to go out. And I covered up for you — she was asking where you were."

Ina scowled. "And what did you tell her?"

"That you were just coming. So you'd better be downstairs when she comes in."

"Huh, I'm not going to hurry myself for her. I don't need this job, you know. Andy and I are going to have our own place soon, just you see."

Jeannie said nothing. As far as she was concerned, Andy and Ina couldn't get their own place soon enough. But privately she doubted whether things were quite as advanced as Ina might like to think. A third horseman's pay didn't have much leeway for saving,

150

especially given that Andy was fond of his beer. Several times Jeannie, up late reading, had heard noises of merriment from the farmyard and had looked out to see Andy and one or two others returning late from the bar in the village, rather the worse for wear.

She went over and picked up Ina's empty cup to take downstairs. Then she stiffened. Poking out from under Ina's pillow were the edges of what looked like a couple of banknotes.

Maybe Ina noticed her reaction because she hastily pulled up the blanket to cover the pillow. "What're you hanging about for?" she snapped. "Haven't you got work to do?"

Jeannie said nothing, but she was thoughtful as she went down to the kitchen. Perhaps she was overreacting, she told herself. Maybe Ina had been saving — but *banknotes?*

Ina came clattering down the stairs a few minutes later, and made a great play of stirring the porridge just as Meg came in. "Oh, good girl, Ina, the men will be in very soon. Jeannie, isn't it time you got the table laid?"

Jeannie flushed at being caught apparently idling, and Meg found herself wondering if she had spoken too harshly. After all, the girl must still be worried about her mother.

"How is Mrs Duncan?" she asked, more kindly, as Jeannie set out the spoons and bowls.

"She's doing well, ma'am," Jeannie replied, her head bowed. She was still smarting under the injustice of Meg's rebuke. She had been the one to get the porridge going, not Ina, and it had been Ina's job to get the table laid. "Sandy and I saw her yesterday, but it will be a while before she's fit to come out."

"And even then she'll have to take things easy," Meg said. "Perhaps you'd like some time off to spend at home and keep an eye on her; make sure she doesn't overdo things. I'm sure we could spare you for a week or two."

"That's very good of you, ma'am." Jeannie spoke with feeling; she had been wondering whether she might ask for time off.

"Well, you just tell me when she's coming out of hospital. You must take a chicken, and some vegetables; she'll need building up. Now here come the men for their breakfast; I'll let you get on."

Jeannie was elated as she served the men their porridge, and several of them teased her about her beaming smile. She wanted to tell Sandy why she was so happy, but she didn't like to with all the others around. She had to wait until they were all finished, and then only when the first horseman had drained his mug of black tea and got to his feet did the others file out after him, leaving Sandy, as the newest and lowliest of the farm workers, as the last to leave the kitchen.

Jeannie caught his arm. "Sandy, you won't believe how kind Mrs Fraser has been!"

She went outside with him to tell him all about it, just as Mr Greig, the postman, came toiling up on his bike.

"Here you are, young Jeannie Duncan, take this bundle of letters off me, will you? And a great fat one there is, from the south of England. It's addressed to

Mistress Fraser — some friend of hers from those parts, I dare say. With a lot of news, by the size of it. Fancy anyone having the time to sit down and write that amount of stuff. Or maybe it's a payment — a large one, I should think."

"I'll take those." Ina had come out of the kitchen as the postman spoke, wiping her hands on her apron. She took the thick envelope and looked at it curiously then turned to Jeannie. "Have you got something to say to your brother? Stay out in the yard then — I don't want to hear it. And while you're at it, you could let the hens out, and they'll need more water."

Leaving them staring after her, she went back inside with the letters. Once inside she looked at the thick envelope, turning it over in her hands. It could contain money. Others had.

The writing on the envelope was in a strong forceful hand, written in black ink. There was a return address on the back, the name *Falconer*, with an address in Kent.

Ina shut the door after Sandy and Jeannie, then she silently closed the door to the front of the house. The kettle was bubbling on the hob; carefully she held the envelope above the spout until she could steam open the envelope. It contained several closely written pages, but, to her intense disappointment, no money.

She stared at the script, trying to decipher it, but it was hard to make out. Reading had never been her strong point. Something about Miss Isobel —

Then the door swung open, and Jeannie came back in. Ina was consumed by guilt. Hastily she stepped over to the range, screwed up the letter and hurled it onto the back of the fire. She held it down with the poker, watching as the words James Falconer had taken such trouble to write went up in smoke. No one would ever read them now.

CHAPTER
FOURTEEN

"What was that?" Jeannie came hurrying over. "What were you burning?"

"Never you mind what it was!" Ina pushed her away so roughly she almost fell in the hearth. "You mind your own business! I'm going to take the mistress her letters right now; you get this table cleared."

She gathered up the rest of the post and hurried out of the kitchen with it, leaving Jeannie staring after her. What was going on? She was almost certain that Ina had burned the letter from England, but why?

She picked up the poker and stirred the mass of burned paper at the back of the fire. It crumbled away as the poker touched it; there was no way it could be deciphered now. She was shocked that Ina could do such a thing, but she really didn't know what she should do about it. She couldn't actually prove that Ina had burned the letter, and if confronted Ina would be sure to deny it.

Jeannie started to clear away the men's breakfast things, then she stopped. Lying on the floor under the table was an envelope. Quickly looking around to make sure no one saw her, she bent down and picked it up. As she thought, it had contained the letter addressed to

Mrs Fraser. So Ina really had opened it and burned the contents!

She stuffed the envelope in her apron pocket. She couldn't risk anyone seeing her with it; she might get the blame for destroying the letter herself. Ina was quite capable of accusing her, and she had no way of proving her innocence. The safest thing would be to throw the envelope on the fire too, but she couldn't bring herself to do it. It might have been something important, something Mrs Fraser was expecting. There may have been money in it — that could be the reason Ina steamed it open. Or perhaps something Ina didn't want her employer to see. Jeannie didn't know what to think.

"Jeannie, can I have a word?" At the sound of Meg's voice calling her name, Jeannie's heart gave a jolt. Could Ina have accused her of destroying the letter already? She could feel her cheeks flaming scarlet as she answered, "Yes, ma'am," and went through to the small room next to the kitchen that Meg used as an office, terribly conscious of the presence of the envelope in her pocket.

Meg looked up as Jeannie came into the room, and was surprised at what she saw. Jeannie looked acutely uncomfortable; one might almost say guilty. As though she was expecting to be accused of something.

She tried to put the girl at ease. "I'm glad to see your brother is settling in so well. It must be nice for you to have him around, especially as this must be a worrying time for you with your mother in hospital."

Jeannie muttered something and poked at the rug with the toe of her shoe. Meg tried again.

156

"I have to go into town this afternoon, and I wondered if you'd like to come with me. There's some shopping to do, then you could drop down to Woolmanhill Hospital to see your mother at visiting time. Dr Nicol said she'd probably be allowed to have visitors today."

"Oh, thank you, ma'am!" Jeannie's face was transformed. "That would be wonderful! I've been so worried about her." She hesitated. "I don't suppose Sandy could come too?"

"I don't think he could be spared today," Meg said, "but he could go next time. Anyway, you wouldn't want to tire your mother; they might not allow too many visitors at once. If you could be ready about two, Dr Nicol's son said he would give us a lift in his motor car."

Jeannie was speechless for a few seconds, then she gasped, "A motor car! I've never been in one before!"

"Well, I'm sure this won't be the last time. I hope you enjoy it." Meg smiled at the girl, then added more seriously, "But, Jeannie, I can't help noticing you look upset. Is something bothering you?"

Jeannie bit her lip. The truthful answer was of course "yes", but she knew she couldn't admit what was really on her mind. So she made do with a half-truth. "I've been very worried about my mother, ma'am," she said quietly. "So I'm very grateful to you for letting me go to see her."

"It's the least I could do," Meg assured her. "And I'm sure that seeing you will do her the world of good.

But don't let me hold you back. Besides, I've got all this post to wade through."

The mention of post brought the colour to Jeannie's face again; she muttered something and fled, leaving Meg thoughtful.

The girl clearly had something on her mind, something she didn't want to share. Meg's thoughts began to take a disturbing turn. Recently she'd noticed a few things going missing. Small sums of cash, a silver spoon, one or two lace handkerchiefs, and then for the past week or two the eggs had been below the usual yield. It all pointed to someone helping themselves, and Meg very much didn't want it to be Jeannie, but her suspicions were aroused. And the girl had a motive; with her mother unable to work for the next few weeks the family needed all the help it could get.

Oh dear, Meg thought. As if I didn't have enough to worry about! I don't want to make any wild accusations, but I'll keep an eye on young Miss Duncan.

That evening, as soon as her work for the day was finished, Jeannie ran up to her little cubbyhole of a room and shut the door. For good measure she hauled her clothes kist against it and wedged it shut; she very definitely didn't want to be disturbed.

It had been a most eventful day. Riding in the motor car had been a real thrill, especially to see everyone staring at them as they bowled along the country roads at what seemed a breakneck speed. And then seeing her mother, very pale and tired-looking, but with a big smile when she saw her daughter — well, that had been simply wonderful.

But all day she'd been conscious of the letter in her pocket, weighing her down like a millstone. When she'd gone into town she'd taken it with her, not daring to leave it in her apron for anyone to find. Now she pulled out the envelope and examined it closely.

It was very crumpled from being carried around all day, but when she smoothed it out the writing, in a bold, forceful hand, was still legible. It was addressed to Meg, and on the back, as the postie had pointed out, was the name Falconer, and a return address.

What to do now? Jeannie sat down on her bed under the skylight, thinking hard. There was only one thing to be done in her opinion. She would have to write to this Mr Falconer — she was sure it was a Mr from the handwriting — and tell him his letter had met with an accident and could he please send another. She wouldn't sign it; in fact she'd ask him please not to mention her letter at all. It was risky, but she felt she simply had to do it.

She opened her kist and drew out some cheap notepaper and envelopes that she had bought for writing to her mother, plus a bottle of ink and a scratchy pen. Then after a few moments' thought she dipped the pen in the ink and began to write.

"Please, I want my mother. Where is she? Can you ask her to come?"

Isobel tossed restlessly against the propped-up pillows, her eyes closed, her breathing fast and shallow.

James Falconer sat by the side of the bed watching her anxiously. "Is there nothing else we can do?" he asked the nurse who was sponging Isobel's brow with tepid water.

"Nothing for the moment. She has to fight this herself." The nurse wrung out the cloth and applied it again, leaving James in an agony of helplessness.

If only Meg was here! Her place was here, at her daughter's side. Two days — no, three now — and there hadn't been a word from her. He'd expected a reply by telegram, but there was not even a letter.

Did she feel so bitterly towards him that she'd thrown away his letter unopened? Maybe it had been a mistake to write the return address on the back. Or could she simply not face seeing him again? Maybe her husband had forbidden her to reply — but what sort of man would bar his wife from the bedside of their sick child?

James stood up and began to pace the floor, hands clasped behind his back. Thoughts crowded in on him. It might have been a mistake to write so much. He'd only meant to state the bare facts, but he'd ended up pouring out so much of his feelings about the loss of his son, his fears for Isobel, and his longing to see Meg again. If her husband had read the letter he would have had every right to feel concerned.

Or perhaps the address had been wrong; Isobel in her weakened state might have made a mistake. And there was always the possibility that the wartime conditions might have delayed the post, or lost it altogether.

160

If Isobel had not been so ill he would have considered taking the train up to Scotland himself, but as it was he didn't dare leave her. Should he send a telegram? Maybe; but if Meg had deliberately chosen to ignore the letter a telegram would be seen as a further unwelcome intrusion. But, dammit, she should be here!

I'll wait and see how it goes with Isobel, he decided. She's holding her own — just — at the moment. I've no right to push myself in where I'm not wanted, but if Isobel's condition deteriorates, I'll send a telegram straightaway.

He went back to the bed and sat down beside it. Isobel, her eyes closed, stretched out her hand and he took it.

"Daddy?" Her voice was a mere thread. "Are you there?"

James bent his head, overcome with emotion. If things had worked out differently he might well have been this girl's father, or even her father-in-law. So if she needed a father figure, he would be it.

"I'm here, darling," he said softly. "I'm right here with you, and I'll stay as long as you need me."

Isobel said nothing but she squeezed his hand. For the first time that day she seemed to be sleeping peacefully. But James knew that when she awoke she'd be looking for her mother again; a mother who, it seemed, had decided to ignore her daughter's desperate need.

"Ellen, where did we put the sulphur ointment? Is it all used up?"

"No, it isn't, there's plenty if you'll only look. Up there above the rolls of bandage."

"Ah, of course!" Dr Jim reached up and grabbed a couple of jars of the yellow ointment. "I need it for Murdo Baird's child — he's come out in a rash. I said I'd take it round this evening."

"And how will Murdo pay for it, seeing as he's been out of work these last two months?" Ellen enquired.

"Ach, I told him not to fret about it. I said he could come and chop a few logs for me when he had the time."

Ellen shook her head, smiling. "Oh, Jim Nicol, you'll never be a rich man but you're a good one. You'd give away the shirt off your back if you thought someone needed it more than you."

Dr Jim laughed. "I'm not sure anyone would thank me for this one. The collar's frayed and the elbows are nearly through." Then he went on more seriously, "I'm sorry, Ellen, love, it hasn't been easy for you. Sometimes I wonder if I shouldn't have taken up the offer of that rich Edinburgh practice. We could have been living in a nice big house in Morningside and —"

"Stop it, Jim!" Ellen laid a finger to his lips. "I wouldn't change a thing! We have everything we need here — a lot more than many of the folk hereabouts have. And you wouldn't have been happy in the city. Go on, admit it."

"I suppose you're right," Dr Jim admitted ruefully. "You usually are."

"And the girls are well settled," Ellen went on. "We've three lovely grandchildren, and Donald is doing

162

well with his business, much better than you thought he would. What more could we want?"

Dr Jim put the ointment down on the table. "All right, since you ask, I'll tell you what I want. The one thing that troubles me is who will take over here when I hang up my stethoscope. There can't be many young doctors who'd want to bury themselves in a quiet country practice where the patients pay you in chopped logs or poached pheasants. It's a worry, Ellen."

"I know, love." Ellen smiled at her husband, but inwardly she was concerned. It wasn't like Jim to talk like this, usually he refused to discuss the possibility of retirement. His hip must be bothering him, she thought anxiously.

She mentioned it to Meg the following day when they met outside the village grocery store. "I think it's on his mind a lot these days. He's very worried that when he calls it a day there'll be no one to take over."

"He'll be a hard act to follow, whoever takes over," Meg said. "Nothing is too much trouble for him. Mind you, he doesn't shrink from speaking his mind when he thinks it necessary."

Ellen laughed. "He certainly doesn't! But enough of our worries, how are things with you? Any solution to your problem with the water supply?"

Meg shook her head. "I'm afraid not." She gave Ellen a brief outline of her meeting with the solicitor that had led to disappointment. "There's an expert coming out this afternoon to look at the wells, see if they can be deepened or if it's worth trying new ones. Maybe he'll have good news."

"I hope so."

"So do I, but if not then we'll have to think of something else. There has to be a way out of this."

"Other than agreeing to become Mrs Dod Grant, you mean?" Ellen said with a wry smile.

"Believe me, that's so much of a last resort that it's not even in sight. There are a lot of options to explore first. Now I must be getting along. Remember me to Dr Jim."

"I will."

Ellen watched Meg walking purposefully away up the hill towards Braeside. She admired the way her friend refused to be beaten, but she couldn't help wondering whether Meg was facing an insurmountable problem.

The sound of a car came towards her round a bend in the road; she stood back to let it pass but it slowed as it came towards her. "Hello, Ma, let me give you a lift home."

"Donald!" Ellen opened the car door and got in beside her son. "What brings you out to these parts? I thought you'd be working. There's nothing wrong, I hope," she added as the car moved off.

"Well, no . . ."

"What is it?" Ellen was troubled. She recognized Donald's tone of old; it was the one he used when he was going to tell her something he didn't think she'd want to hear. "Stop the car, son. I think you'd better tell me about it, whatever it is."

Donald stopped the car in a gateway and turned to face her. "There's no hiding anything from you, is

164

there, Ma? Well, I suppose it would be a good idea to tell you first before I give Dad the news."

"Oh, son, what is it?" Ellen was really worried now. "Is there some problem with the business? Do you owe money? Your father and I will do all we can to help." Even as she spoke she had to admit to herself that finding spare cash to help if Donald had debts would not be easy. Even harder would be breaking the news to her husband.

So it was a relief when Donald said with a laugh, "No, it's nothing like that. In fact the business is going pretty well at the moment."

"Then what?" Ellen's mind raced. Could he have got himself in trouble with some girl? Or fallen foul of the law?

"Why must you think it's bad news?" Donald said. "Some parents would be delighted to hear what I'm going to tell you. It would make them very proud."

And suddenly Ellen knew. "Oh, Donald! You're going to join the army."

"Yes, Mother. In fact I've already done it. I signed up today."

"But your asthma — they rejected you because of it — oh don't say you lied about it?"

"Other people have lied to join the army. Lots lie about their age, so why not this? And the asthma's not that bad."

Ellen said nothing, but she remembered the long nights when they'd sat up with Donald as he'd fought for breath. What would it be like for him in the trenches, where conditions were appalling even for the able-bodied?

There was a catch in her voice as she asked, "Why, son? Why now?"

Donald looked away. "I got another white feather yesterday. I can't stand being called a coward, Mother. I'm not, and I want to prove it."

"I know you're not, Donald," Ellen said quietly. "You don't need to do this to prove it."

"It's too late now; I've signed up. I have to go tomorrow —"

"So soon!"

"'Fraid so. But it's only to training camp for starters. I was coming home to say goodbye to you and Dad."

Ellen couldn't speak. She should be proud of her son, she knew, because he was going off to serve his country, but if she was honest with herself she knew she would do anything just to keep him safe at home.

James Falconer picked up the letter with the Scottish postmark and turned it over in his hands. The address was written in careful copperplate, not at all as he remembered Meg's hasty scribble, but it wasn't impossible that she might have changed her style over the last twenty years. At least she had written, and not before time!

He was surprised at the depth of emotion he felt just looking at the letter. To think that he and Meg were communicating again after all those years! His pulse quickened as he slit open the envelope and took out the single sheet it contained, but after reading a few lines his brows knit in a frown. It wasn't from Meg at all.

Dear Mr Falconer
I regret that the letter you recently sent to Mrs Fraser of Braehead has met with an accident before she was able to read it. Please could you send another at your earliest convenience. Mrs Fraser knows nothing about the letter, nor does she know that I have written to you. Forgive me for not signing this.

So that explained Meg's silence! She'd never even received his letter, and she didn't know that Isobel was with him or anything about her daughter's illness. He'd condemned her as callous and uncaring, but she hadn't even known. A wave of relief washed over him; he hadn't wanted to believe ill of Meg, and now it seemed he had no reason to.

But what had happened to his letter, and who had written this? One of her other children, perhaps? Her husband? Or, more likely, a postal worker who had damaged the original in some way and didn't want to own up? Clearly someone with an education, because the letter was well written and correctly spelt. It was a mystery.

He felt a stab of anger against the unknown person. Did they not realize this could be a life or death matter? Their meddling might yet have serious consequences. He vowed that he would get to the bottom of this and make sure whoever was at fault was found out and brought to account.

Meanwhile, what to do now? Do as the anonymous writer suggested, he supposed, and write again. Perhaps it was a good thing; he had let his emotions run away with him first time round. This time he would be more circumspect, and keep strictly to the facts of the matter.

As he picked up his pen there was a knock at the study door, and before he could call "Come in", the door opened and the nurse stood there.

"I'm very sorry to disturb you, sir, but Miss Fraser has taken a turn for the worse. I think you should come up."

James was out of his chair before she had finished speaking. He took the stairs two at a time and hurried into Isobel's room, where the doctor was beside her.

"How is she?"

The doctor looked grave. "Her temperature has rocketed, and as you can see her breathing is laboured. I have to say I'm gravely concerned. The next few hours could be critical."

James silently cursed whoever it was that had prevented his letter from arriving. Were it not for them Meg could have been here by now at her daughter's side; but now it might be too late.

But he refused to let himself think like that. "I'll telegraph her mother," he said tersely, and left the room.

Later that day Will came hurrying into the dairy where Meg was skimming some milk. She looked up, startled, as he clattered in.

168

"My, someone's in a hurry! Are you so glad to be out of school? Did you have a good day?"

Will ignored her question. "There's a telegram for you. The boy's just brought it."

Meg felt a jolt of alarm. Telegrams were invariably bad news. She remembered that ghastly day when she'd received one to say that Alistair had been killed in action — it had been so abrupt, giving her no time to prepare herself.

With an effort she forced herself to stay calm for Will's sake; she could see that he was worried. She rinsed her hands and wiped them on an old towel. "Right, thanks, I'll come at once. Did you give the boy sixpence?"

"Er —"

"All right, I'll do it. I expect he'll be waiting to see if there's any reply."

She walked back to the house, talking inconsequentially to Will about the day's events, relieved to see him start to relax. The telegram boy was in the kitchen warming himself by the range and Meg was pleased to find that Jeannie had given him a mug of cocoa. He handed her the envelope.

"Thank you. If you'd be good enough to wait, there might be a reply. I'll take it through to the parlour."

She realized it was rather pointless going off to read it in private, when the postmistress had probably relayed its contents round the neighbourhood already, especially if it was bad news. But she didn't want to have an audience when she opened it and read what it contained.

She went over to the window, opened the envelope and read. *Isobel dangerously ill STOP Staying at my house STOP Please come at once STOP James Falconer.*

The paper fluttered from Meg's fingers on to the floor; she clutched the edge of the windowsill for support. She couldn't believe what she had just read, there must be some mistake. Feverishly she scrabbled on the floor, and spread out the flimsy piece of paper, reading it over and over again.

It was incredible. Why was Isobel with James Falconer? Why hadn't she been in touch? And *dangerously ill* . . .

"I must go to her." Meg, distracted, spoke out loud. "I must —"

"Mother, what is it?" Will ran into the room and took her arm, plainly at a loss to see his mother, usually in control of any situation, so obviously upset and unsure of herself.

Wordlessly Meg held out the telegram to him, not trusting herself to speak. Will glanced at it, then he looked up, clearly confused. "I don't understand. Who is this James Falconer person, and why is Isobel there?"

Meg felt for a chair and sat down heavily. "He's the father of the man she was engaged to. You remember us telling you about him? David Falconer. He was killed, poor soul, or rather reported missing. It amounts to the same thing."

"Yes, but why is she there? This address is somewhere in Kent. I thought she was in France?"

"So did I. I can't imagine why she's there, unless she went to visit the family and then was taken ill."

"Dangerously ill. Oh, Mother, poor Isobel. What can we do?"

Faced with her son's distress, Meg made herself calm down. She took a deep breath. "Isobel's in good hands. David's father will look after her. But all the same this sounds serious. I think I should go down to be with her, and the sooner the better."

"I can cope," Will said eagerly. "Don't worry about anything."

Meg reached out and took his hand in hers. "You're a good lad, Will. All the same I'd feel easier if I asked someone — maybe the minister's daughter — to come and stay here while I'm away. Just to keep an eye on the house," she went on before Will could protest. "After all, you'll be away at school during the day."

"But I could take time off!"

"There's no need for that. Alec the foreman will look after things on the farm, and he might be glad of your help, but I can't see you coping with laundry, or keeping the housemaids in order. Can you? No, you're best at school; it will keep your mind off things."

Will looked abashed. "Well, if you say so."

"I do. And I don't know what I'm going to find when I get down there." Meg's tone was matter-of-fact, but inwardly she was desperately worried about her daughter. "I may have to stay down there for some time," she went on, "so I have to make sure that everything is taken care of here at Braehead. I'll leave a note of the address in case you need to get in touch with me about anything."

Will marvelled at his mother's composure. So many women, he was sure, would have dissolved into hysterics, or panicked, but here was his mother speaking as though a daughter's dangerous illness was an everyday occurrence. He wasn't to know the mental anguish that Meg was hiding from him.

"When are you going?" he asked.

"I'll get the overnight sleeper. I think it leaves about ten. I'll get Alec to drive me into town. So I'd better go upstairs and pack."

"Are you sure you don't want me to come with you? It's an awful long way."

"I won't notice, I'll be asleep," Meg assured him. "Now I'd better write a reply to that telegram so that the boy can get back with it."

She took pen and paper, and after a moment's thought, wrote, *Expect me tomorrow STOP Meg Fraser*

Succinct and to the point. She went through to the kitchen with Will and gave the boy her reply and the money to pay for it, plus sixpence for himself. Then she went upstairs to pack.

Once up in her room, putting clothes into a small suitcase, the enormity of what she was doing suddenly hit home to Meg. Not only was she going down to be with Isobel — and please God I'm not too late, she thought desperately — but she was going to meet her former sweetheart, the man she'd parted from with such bitterness all those years ago. How on earth was she going to face him?

CHAPTER
FIFTEEN

Meg stepped out of the Aberdeen sleeper onto the cold drizzle of a London dawn, stifling a yawn. Although she had managed to get some sleep she felt drained, and her journey was by no means over.

Even at this early hour the station was busy and she was reminded how much she had appreciated her move to the country away from the hustle and bustle of city life. She started to look for the entrance to the Underground. She wasn't looking forward to this part of the journey, as she had always felt claustrophobic down in the tunnels. But it had to be faced; she had to change stations and this was the quickest way to do it. There was no time to waste in getting to her daughter's side. She picked up her bag and set off in the direction of the sign.

Suddenly she heard her name called. It was so unexpected that at first she took no notice, thinking she must have misheard. But then it came again. "Mrs Fraser?"

There was no mistaking it this time. And no mistaking the voice. Meg's emotions spiralled, she felt suddenly weak at the knees, but somehow she kept control, somehow she turned to face the questioner, her face a polite mask. "Yes, I'm Mrs Fraser."

Then she caught her breath. After more than twenty years, she was standing face to face with James Falconer. She would have recognized him anywhere, even though his dark hair was streaked with grey and there were lines of tension round his mouth and eyes. For a few moments everything else ceased to exist; she didn't know what to say, what to think even. Her mouth was dry.

At last she managed to find words. "I — I didn't expect you to meet me. How did you know —"

"I thought you'd be on the Aberdeen sleeper; it seemed the obvious thing for you to do. I decided it would be quickest if I met the train and take you from here by car. Anyway, I know you always used to hate the Underground."

Meg said nothing as the implication of his words hit home. He'd remembered that. So he hadn't forgotten her completely. There must have been times over the last twenty years when he'd thought back to their time together, perhaps with affection? But she was treading on dangerous ground. She mustn't allow herself to think like this. Isobel was her only concern.

"Thank you," she said quietly. "How is Isobel?"

James bent down and picked up her bag, so she couldn't see his expression, but concern was evident in his voice. "She's holding her own," he answered, "but we shouldn't waste time. We have a fair way to go."

Meg felt ice cold. James's calm words affected her more deeply than a hysterical outburst would have done; she instantly recognized the gravity of the situation. Without further comment she fell in step with him and together they walked out of the station to where a gleaming black car stood waiting, a chauffeur at the wheel.

"This is yours?" Meg asked, instantly regretting the question. Of course it was — what a stupid thing to say! But how ironic, she thought, as she scrambled in. Her parents had always looked down on James as beneath their notice, but it seemed that he had risen far beyond their expectations.

James got in beside her and directed the chauffeur to set off. He turned to Meg. "You must be wondering how she came to be at my house. She literally turned up on the doorstep, tired and ill. She'd been meaning to stay with friends but there was some sort of misunderstanding, I think, and as she had my address from my son she saw me as a last resort."

"It was very good of you to help." Meg's response was heartfelt. "I'm so grateful to you."

"There's no need for gratitude — it's the least I could do. In happier circumstances I would have welcomed her to my house as my son's bride."

Silence fell between them. Meg could not trust herself to speak and she felt that James understood.

When they at last drew up outside his house she was more prepared for its size and grandeur, but even so she couldn't help wondering what her parents would have made of it all. The journey had passed mostly in silence; apart from a few courteous enquiries as to her journey, James had left her alone with her thoughts.

"You'll want to go straight up to her?" he suggested as they went inside.

"Yes, please." Meg allowed the maid to take her coat and hat and followed James up the wide staircase to Isobel's room. Her heart was pounding and she was very apprehensive as to what she might find, but she forced herself to keep up a semblance of calm as she entered the room.

A nurse was sitting by the bed; she looked up as they entered. "She's still feverish, sir," she said in answer to James's query, with a curious glance at Meg.

"I'm sure you're doing all you can. This lady is her mother, Mrs Fraser. She's travelled all night to be here."

Meg shook hands with the nurse, sensing that James was feeling the need to make excuses for her. She didn't know why. Surely she'd taken the quickest means of transport that she could? But that wasn't important. Right now she wanted to see her daughter.

She stepped forward to the bedside, then she was unable to hold back an exclamation of horror. Isobel was tossing restlessly, her face flushed. Her eyes were half open but she seemed to see nothing. "How long has she been like this?" Meg demanded.

The nurse spoke up before James could reply. "Almost a week, madam. Mr Fraser wrote to you immediately, but there was no reply."

"A week! But I knew nothing of this! I didn't get any letter!" Meg stared at James. "Why, I could have been —" She was going to say "too late" but she choked on the words.

"It's not important." James came over and stood beside her. "It's wartime; things are difficult." He turned to the nurse. "I happen to know that the letter got lost in the post. The main thing is that Mrs Fraser is here now. That will do Isobel more good than any amount of medicine."

Meg sat down, her eyes fixed on her daughter's face. James was right. The important thing now was to be with Isobel and nurse her back to health. She was going to concentrate on that to the exclusion of everything else.

"You must eat something," James said. He turned to the nurse and gave quiet instructions. She nodded and left the room.

"What is the matter with her?" Meg asked in a low voice. "Is this the influenza we keep hearing about?"

"I'm afraid so. Complicated in her case by the poor conditions she's been living in out in France — it's weakened her system. But she's a fighter, I've learned that in the time I've spent with her. She'll not give up easily."

Meg waited tensely. She almost expected him to add "unlike her mother". He said nothing but she could guess he was thinking it. And he'd be right. She had given up on him so easily all those years ago. But since then she'd changed so much. If only she could make him understand that she wasn't the weak-willed person he remembered.

Tension stretched between them, taut as a wire. The nurse returned with a plate of sandwiches and a pot of

177

tea. Meg made herself eat, but the food went down untasted. All her attention was fixed on Isobel.

"Darling, I'm here," she whispered. "You're going to be all right. We'll get you well again."

Then Isobel's eyes opened and she looked around wildly, struggling to speak. "Daddy —" she got out at last. "Where are you —"

Her eyes fell on James, and she smiled. "You're there, I knew you'd come." She stretched out a hand to him. "Don't leave me."

James took her hand in his. "I won't leave you, sweetheart."

He spoke quietly to Meg. "I'm sorry, I don't mean to take your husband's place but she doesn't realize who I am. It seems kinder to let her believe her father's here." He leaned forward. "Isobel, there's someone else here. It's your mother, darling. Look here she is."

"Mother?" Isobel frowned. "Where? I can't see her, it's too dark —"

"I'm here, love, right here." Meg took Isobel's other hand, holding it as tightly as she dared. "I'm going to look after you till you're better."

Later she couldn't remember how long she sat there, Isobel's hand clasped in hers. She only knew that when James touched her shoulder and said, "It's all right, she's sleeping now," she was so stiff that she could hardly get up from the chair.

Dazedly she said, "Is that a good sign?"

"Good? It's wonderful. It's the first really peaceful sleep she's had in days. I think she may have turned the corner."

178

"Oh." Meg looked up at him and to her amazement she saw that his eyes were wet with tears. Instinctively she reached out and put her arms round him and they clung together soundlessly for a few long moments. A cough from the nurse brought them back to reality.

"I'm sorry." James's arms dropped to his sides and he stepped back.

"That's all right." Meg felt awkward; she knew she was blushing, something she hadn't done in years. "I'm just so relieved," she excused.

"You'll want to get in touch with your husband."

"My husband?" Meg stared at him, then she understood. "Of course. How were you to know? Alistair was killed in the early weeks of the war. I've been a widow over three years now."

"Oh." There was an awkward silence, then James said, "I'm very sorry."

"Thank you. And I was so sorry to hear about your son. These are terrible times."

"Indeed they are. And all the more reason to make sure that Isobel here pulls through safely."

It seemed to Will that everywhere he went people wanted to know about his mother and sister. Everyone had heard about Meg's dash down south to be with Isobel, and rumours were flying round about the girl's condition.

"She's out of danger," Will repeated for the umpteenth time in reply to a concerned query from the village grocer. "But my mother is going to stay down there with her for a while yet because she's still very weak."

"And will she be coming back home then? Surely she won't be going back to that hospital in France?"

"I don't know," Will replied truthfully. "Perhaps they'll want her back to nurse the wounded soldiers. But she'll have to get back on her feet first."

"Nay, she won't have to go back," someone else put in. "Isn't the war going to be over soon? Well before Christmas, they say."

"And when have we heard that before?" the grocer snapped back. "Every year since 1914. So why should 1918 be any different?"

Will left them to it. He picked up the bag of groceries and went out into the cold autumn air. He wondered when his mother would be coming home, and whether she would indeed bring Isobel along with her. It had been a great relief to hear that Isobel was making a good recovery, but his mother's latest letter had warned that it would be a slow process.

He was looking forward to having his mother home again; although he wouldn't have admitted it, he missed her very much. Alec the foreman was running the farm efficiently, and the minister's unmarried daughter ruled the household with a rod of iron, but things weren't the same. And Will had discovered something that worried him very much.

In Meg's absence he'd taken the opportunity of looking through some of the paperwork in the farm office. He'd felt a bit guilty about it, but, after all, he'd

180

said to himself, he should be aware of what's going on, just in case.

But what he'd found had shocked him to the core. He'd known about the water problem and the fact that Dod Grant was threatening to block up the culvert that ran through his land, but Will had never realized just what a catastrophic effect that would have on Braehead. Meg had never revealed the true extent of the problem. Will gasped as he read through the correspondence with the solicitor, the depressing results of the surveys, the accountant's forecast of the disastrous effect on the farm's profits. Why, it could mean the end of everything.

But how wonderful if he could find a way out of the problem! If his mother could come back from London to find everything solved and the future of the farm assured. The more he thought it through, the more convinced he became that he could sort something out.

Dod Grant was a notorious misogynist, everyone knew that. So it was no wonder that he disdained to negotiate with Meg Fraser. But he might be prepared to do business with her son, who, although he was as yet underage, was after all the future owner of Braehead. Perhaps Dod might accept an offer of some land, or some cash arrangement. He surely must have his price — it was just that Meg had failed to find it.

And there was no time like the present, Will thought suddenly, as he saw Dod coming out of the smithy at the end of the lane, leading a large black horse. It would be so easy to fall in step with him and start up a conversation. He quickened his pace and soon caught up with the pair.

"Good day to you, Mr Grant!"

Dod turned, scowling. "What the — Oh, it's yoursel', young Master Fraser. And what might ye be wantin' wi' me?"

"Er, well, nothing really. Just to pass the time of day, you know."

"So? Well, consider it passed, lad, and you be gettin' up off home after your hard day at the school. Time you were in for your tea, I'm thinkin'."

This wasn't how Will had planned it. He felt at a loss, until he noticed the black horse was limping. "The smith hasn't done a very good job for you, Mr Grant. Your horse is still limping, see? Shouldn't you take him back?"

Dod stopped. "Well, thank ye for pointing that out tae me, laddie," he said with heavy sarcasm. "I'd never have noticed that mysel'."

"But aren't you going to do something about it?"

"Indeed I am not! Why do you think I'm takin' the animal away? The price that man's chargin' is ridiculous! Daylight robbery! I'm no' payin' that!"

"So what are you going to do? You can't leave the poor horse like this."

"Nor will I. He's needed on the plough in the morn. I'll take him up to the smithy beyond the kirk, see what they can offer me. Bound to be a better deal than what I'd get back there."

Will said nothing. He knew that the other smithy did not have a good reputation and his mother would never

182

use it. He felt sorry for the horse, clearly in pain and having to trudge the extra distance so that his master could make a small saving. But maybe this was the opening he needed.

"You're known as one who drives a hard bargain, Mr Grant," he began.

"That I am and rightly so." Dod looked at Will with narrowed eyes. "If there were more like me there wouldnae be the terrible high prices we have to put up with. But what of it?"

Will plunged on. "I was thinking about the culvert. I know it's an imposition to you, having it cross your land, but if we made you a substantial offer —"

Dod threw back his head and laughed, causing the horse to shy nervously. He jerked on its rope. "Why, has your mama set you onto me?" he asked with a sneer. "Did she think that the pleadin' of her child would soften my hard heart?"

"No, of course not!" Will flashed back. "She knows nothing of this! She's been down in Kent with Isobel this past week."

"So this is your idea then? A wee project of your own?"

"You could say that. Braehead will be mine one day, and I'd be prepared to make you an offer."

Dod laughed again. "An offer! Hark at him! And have you any idea of the sort of offer I'd be minded to accept? Has your precious mother told you that, then?"

"No, but —"

"Well, hear this." Dod took a step closer to Will and stared up into his face. "How would you feel about having me as a stepdad? How about it? Could you persuade your mother to accept me?"

"What?" Will was astounded. For a moment he was completely bereft of speech, then he burst out, "No, it's impossible!"

"Why? Is my land not as good as hers? Better indeed, for I've plenty of water. As she could have if she'd only see sense. Put a word in for me, laddie, and I could show my gratitude."

"Why, you —" Will saw red. Dropping the groceries he rushed at Dod, fists clenched. Dod stepped back and collided with the horse, which reared in fright. One of its hooves struck Dod a glancing blow; he dropped to the ground, stunned. A group of men, just coming out of the smithy behind them, ran up.

"What's going on here? Will Fraser, what have you done?"

One man calmed the horse while two of them helped Dod to his feet. He stared wildly at Will. "He attacked me! Knocked me to the ground! You saw it!"

"It wasn't me," Will said angrily, "though I'd have liked to. It was the horse, the poor beast. You frightened it."

"You saw what happened!" Dod shouted at the men. "Why, he might have killed me if you hadn't been here. He was the one frightened the horse. He should be locked up."

The men were muttering amongst themselves; Will realized with a sick feeling that some of them appeared to be taking Dod's side. They couldn't have seen what happened, he thought desperately. They must just have seen Dod fall to the ground and jumped to the wrong conclusion.

No one saw the pony and trap approach until a well-known voice broke in on them. "Seems like my services might be needed here. Dod Grant with a bleeding head — how did that happen?"

Will spun round in relief to see Dr Jim looking down at him. "The horse knocked him over. It —"

"It did nothing of the sort!" Dod interrupted. "It was Will Fraser that knocked me down. Came at me like a maniac, he did. The lad can't be right in the head!"

"Did anyone see what happened?" Dr Jim asked, looking round.

No one answered. "Well, it's just your word against his," Dr Jim said to Dod, "but I have to say that looks like a hoof mark to me. You'll be wanting me to have a look at it for you?"

"And get a fat fee out o' me? Think again, Doc."

Dr Jim swept him a scathing glance. "In that case I'll be wishing you good day. Will, I'm going your way. Let me give you a lift up to the farm."

Will accepted with alacrity. He grabbed the bag of groceries and jumped up into the trap. Dr Jim clicked his tongue to the pony and they set off at a brisk trot.

"So, what have you been up to, my lad?" the doctor asked. "Getting yourself into a spot of trouble, it seems."

Will's temper flared. "You should have heard what he said about my mother! He had no right to speak of her like that!"

"So you planted him one, did you?"

"No, I didn't, but I wish I had."

"Calm down, lad, that sort of talk won't help you. Dod Grant is not a good person to cross. If it should come to taking sides I guess most of those fellows would be prepared to back him up in his story."

"But it's not true!"

"Steady, lad, you'll scare the pony if you shout like that. I'm not deaf, you know. And I'm prepared to believe you, but I didn't see what went on."

"So what will happen now?" Will felt apprehensive. What if his mother got to hear of this? What if she arrived home to find he'd been carted off to jail for assault and battery? She already had enough worries on her plate with Isobel, not to mention the problem with the farm water supply, which he had probably just made worse.

"Don't worry." Dr Jim seemed to be reading his thoughts. "Your mother won't know anything of this. I'll have a word with those chaps. I can get them to see sense, I've no doubt. Most of them owe me a few favours."

They pulled up at the gates of Braehead and Will jumped down. "Thanks, Dr Nicol."

"Think nothing of it. I'm doing it for your mother. Things are hard enough for her at the moment without her precious boy getting himself into bother. Any news, by the way?"

"Of Isobel? Yes, it's good news, we had a letter yesterday. She's over the worst but she's very weak. Mother is staying down there for a while; she'll let us know when she's coming back."

186

"Good." Dr Jim leaned down and shook a finger at Will. "Now the best thing you can do, my lad, is keep your nose clean until she comes back. Don't give her anything else to worry about. Will you promise me that?"

"Of course. And thanks."

Will stood by the gate until the trap disappeared round the bend then he went inside. He had meant what he said about keeping out of trouble, but all the same he wasn't sure whether it wouldn't come to find him. There had been a distinctly ugly look on Dod Grant's face, and Will couldn't help feeling that he hadn't heard the last of things.

CHAPTER
SIXTEEN

"Mum, you're out of bed! This is wonderful!" Jeannie Duncan ran up to her mother where she sat in a chair by her hospital bed. "You're looking so much better."

"And I'm feeling better. I'd go home tomorrow if they'd let me, but they're talking about another week at least. Would you believe it?"

"You have to go along with what they say." Jeannie pulled up another chair and sat down. "We don't want you overdoing it again and ending up back here."

Her mother shuddered. "No chance of that! Why, I've never been ordered about so much in my life. Do this, do that, eat up your greens, time for a blanket bath. And the poor nurses, they're rushed off their feet. That sister is a demon."

"Don't forget they've got you well again," Jeannie chided gently. "They're only trying to do what's best."

"Well, maybe," Mrs Duncan assented grudgingly. Then she brightened up. "But tell me all your news. You know how I love to hear what's going on outside these walls. How's young Master Will?"

She smiled encouragingly at her daughter as she spoke, but Jeannie's heart sank. She knew how much her mother wanted her and Will Fraser to get together, and the knowledge made her feel awkward with Will. It had made her turn down his invitation to the Saturday night dance, for fears of starting rumours that she was out to get him. She didn't want him to feel in any way that she was throwing herself at him with a view to raising her status in society. All the same, she had to admit she genuinely liked him and she knew he valued her help with his schoolwork.

"He's well enough, Mum," she said vaguely. "I don't see that much of him these days, and of course he has his mother and sister to think of."

"Oh, poor Mrs Fraser, having to stay down there in England. Mind you, that's where she's from, isn't it, though you'd never think it, a nice lady like her. But how is Miss Isobel?"

"On the mend from what I hear. Mrs Fraser's hoping to bring her back up to Braehead before too long."

"She should never have left the place. If she'd wanted to be a nurse there's plenty of opportunity here without having to go abroad. Much safer too."

Jeannie said nothing. She knew that once her mother got an idea into her head it was hard to shift. She tried to change the subject.

"Sandy's doing well, Mum. They're giving him more responsibility now that one of the ploughmen has a broken ankle. The foreman is very pleased with him."

Her mother sniffed. "Well, we'll see about that once I'm out of here. I never wanted that lad to go into farming."

"But he loves it, Mum. It's what he's always wanted to do."

"It was what your father did, and look where it got us."

There was no answer to that. No point in Jeannie trying to argue that her father's heart had never been in farming the way Sandy's was. She could only hope that when Mrs Fraser got back she would support Sandy in his wish to stay on at Braehead, and somehow convince her mother that it was in all their interests to let him carry on.

She changed the subject once more to more commonplace matters, and chatted away until it was nearly time for the end of visiting. "Well, I'll be getting back now. Miss Gillespie from the manse is in charge at Braehead while Mrs Fraser's away, and she's terribly particular. Everything has to be exactly so."

"Well, don't you worry your head about her, Jeannie, love," her mother said, "because you won't have to bear with her much longer."

"No, thank heaven, Mrs Fraser will soon be back."

"That wasn't what I was meaning. I'll be out of here soon and then I'll be needing you back with me."

Jeannie stared at her mother. "But — but Mrs Fraser depends on me!"

"You might like to think so, Jeannie, but she can easy get another girl to help her in the house. There's plenty looking for work. No, lass, your place is at home with me. I can't do the heavy lifting any more, and I can't afford to give up the laundry work."

The bell for the end of visiting rang out before Jeannie could say anything; as it was, she was completely lost for words. It felt as though her whole world was threatened. Mrs Fraser had talked about letting her continue her studies; realize her dream of becoming a teacher. She'd even begun to believe it might happen. Now it all seemed as far off as ever.

Subdued, she kissed her mother goodbye and joined the throng of people filing out of the wards and down the stairs. Tears pricked at her eyelids, but she blinked them back. It wouldn't do to be seen crying here.

"Why, Jeannie Duncan, it's good to see you! How's your mother doing?"

Jeannie looked up to see the smiling face of Mrs Nicol, Dr Jim's wife. She swallowed hard. "She's doing fine, thank you."

"Are you sure? You don't look too certain. Here, take this handkerchief." The tears that Jeannie couldn't hold back were rolling down her cheeks now, and Ellen Nicol was genuinely concerned. "Your mother hasn't taken a turn for the worse, has she?" she asked gently.

Jeannie shook her head. "No, she's much better. She hopes to be out in a week or so."

"So what's upsetting you, my dear? Can I be of any help?"

Jeannie couldn't stop herself. The whole story came pouring out, there and then, as they walked along the hospital corridor.

"And I shouldn't be feeling like this," she finished miserably. "I should be overjoyed that my mother will soon be out of hospital, but really I'm dreading it because then I'll have to go back to being a drudge. There's no way round it. She needs my help, but it's the end of all my hopes."

Ellen put an arm round Jeannie's shaking shoulders. "Don't give up, my dear," she advised. "There's a solution to this problem — all we have to do is look for it."

But she couldn't help feeling that she sounded much more confident than she felt.

Isobel put down her knife and fork and looked up triumphantly at her mother. "There! A clean plate! Don't you think I'm doing well?"

Meg smiled. "You're doing splendidly, darling. I'm very proud of you. You're looking so much better."

"So how long before I can go back?"

"Back where?"

"Why, to France, of course. They need all the nursing staff they can get."

"But, Isobel, surely you heard what the doctor said —"

"I heard all right! He hasn't a clue! He should see what people have to go through out in France. A mere dose of flu is no excuse for shirking one's duty."

"Darling, what you had was no 'mere dose of flu'. You were gravely ill —"

"And now I'm better. So I want to go back as soon as possible."

Meg sighed to herself. She could see that Isobel had inherited her own pigheadedness, and it was going to be very difficult persuading her that she was in no fit state to even think of resuming her nursing.

Perhaps James's advice would carry more weight, Meg thought. But ever since she had arrived from

Scotland, James had hardly been in the house. He had left early each morning before she came down for breakfast and only reappeared late in the evening. Even then he spent most of his time locked away in his study.

He claimed pressures of business as his excuse, but Meg was sure she knew better. That awful moment when she had stepped into his arms on the first day of her visit, overwhelmed with relief that Isobel seemed to have turned the corner, that was clearly the reason behind James's absence. He was deliberately distancing himself from her. Whenever they did meet he was super-formal, addressing her as Mrs Fraser and engaging her only in superficial conversation. It was as if he was afraid that she might still harbour hopes of regaining his affection.

Well, Meg thought, he need have no fears on that score. As soon as Isobel is well enough, we will leave for Scotland together. In fact the sooner I'm back on the farm the better — there are a hundred and one things to be seen to.

But the difficulty was going to be convincing Isobel. And to do that James's help would be needed. She would have to approach him as soon as possible, and hope that he did not misinterpret her motives.

She made up her mind to do it that very evening, but in the end James made the first move. As she was leaving Isobel's room after settling her down for the night, he came out of his study and beckoned to her.

"Mrs Fraser, could I have a word?"

"Certainly." Meg followed him into the room, outwardly composed but inwardly wondering why he wanted to speak to her. It must be about Isobel, surely, but as she took the seat he offered she saw that his face was troubled. Did he have bad news? she asked herself, with mounting agitation. Could the doctor have told him something about Isobel's condition?

"What is it?" she asked urgently as he sat down opposite her. "Please tell me straight, I can bear it whatever it is."

James steepled his fingers together, resting his elbows on the desk. For a few long seconds he said nothing, then he raised his head and looked directly into her eyes.

"It's David. They think there's a chance he might be alive."

Meg could scarcely believe what she was hearing. "But — but that's wonderful news! After all this time! How — I mean, where — and, oh, there are so many questions! You must be so thrilled. And Isobel, she'll be ecstatic." Then she paused. James wasn't looking overjoyed; far from it.

"I wouldn't tell her just yet," he said quietly. "The thing is, it's not one hundred per cent certain that it really is David. You see, he was involved in an explosion, one of those ghastly mines, and apparently it tore his clothing to shreds. There was no identification on him, it was all destroyed. And he had lost his memory — hardly surprising really — so there was no way of knowing who he was. Fortunately he's beginning to remember things and they're starting to piece the story together."

"So where is he now?" Meg asked.

"He was behind enemy lines, in a French hospital run by nuns. The authorities got to hear of it through the Red Cross. Once he began to get his memory back they had him transferred to a British military hospital somewhere in Picardy. These sort of exchanges of the wounded go on from time to time. Civilized, isn't it?" He laughed cynically. "Then when they've had enough of being civilized they start shooting and blowing each other up again. Unbelievable!"

"But what about David?" Meg prompted.

"I'm sorry, I was letting my frustration run away with me. Well, I've been informed that if David is well enough he'll be brought home."

Meg picked up on the telling phrase. "*If* he's well enough?"

James took a long slow breath. "He was very badly injured. The head injury that caused the memory loss wasn't the only thing. It seems his legs were severely affected; at first they thought he would lose at least one of them. They managed to save them both, thank God, but they've warned me that he might never walk again."

Meg was stunned. She stared down at her hands, clasped tightly in her lap. "That's appalling," she whispered. "It's wonderful that he's alive, but —"

"But he'll never again be the dashing young man who went away to fight for his country? No, he won't, and the sad thing is there are hundreds, thousands like him."

Silence fell between them, then James spoke again. "And what of Isobel? How will she feel when she learns that the man she wanted to marry might spend the rest of his life in a wheelchair? Not to mention the head injury; we don't know what effect that may have had." He buried his face in his hands.

"James." Meg got to her feet and went round the desk to him, resting one hand on his shoulder. "You mustn't let yourself think like this. There's no point in speculating. Things might not be as bad as you think. Look, they've already succeeded in saving his legs, he's getting his memory back — all these are positive things. Hold on to them. And as for Isobel, well, I can't speak for her, but I'm as sure as I can be that if she truly loves your son this will make no difference whatsoever to her."

James reached up and took her hand in his, squeezing it gently. "Thank you." He paused a moment, then he added, "I'm glad you're here, Meg. I have to admit I wasn't looking forward to seeing you again — too many bad memories — but I'm glad you're with us now. I don't know if I could have stood this on my own."

Meg. That was the first time he had used her given name since they had parted all those years ago. To hear him say it again under such poignant circumstances was almost more than Meg could bear, She bit down on her lip to steady herself, then she said, "I'm sure you could, but I'm happy to be here and help share it. And James —"

"Yes?"

"Have you noticed you've just called me Meg again? Can we drop the 'Mrs Fraser' and 'Mr Falconer' bit? It's so artificial. Surely after all this time, and in such circumstances, we can simply be friends and support each other, and call each other by our first names? What do you think?"

James looked up with a wry smile. "You're right. I'm sorry. Meg it is then, or do you answer to Margaret these days?"

"Most people call me Meg."

"Then so shall I. I'm sorry about the formality; I didn't know how to approach you, I suppose. But the past is behind us now. We've both moved on."

Meg paused only fractionally before she said, "So we have. And the important thing now is the young folk. What are we going to do? I can't help thinking it would be best not to say anything to Isobel just yet."

"That's what I was thinking too. She's still getting over a serious illness; terrible news like this could set her back. And, of course, there's still the outside chance that this isn't David. It would be cruel to raise her hopes and then have to dash them again."

"How soon will we know?"

"Very soon, I hope. I'm going over there tomorrow."

"What?"

"I've made arrangements to start first thing in the morning. I'm not waiting for the army to get round to shipping him back, I'm going to bring him home myself. The only thing is I don't know how long I'll be. How do you feel about staying here with Isobel? I'm very conscious of keeping you away from the farm."

Meg didn't hesitate. "My place is with my daughter. The farm will be fine; I have a very competent foreman who's been dying to have complete responsibility for a good while now. I just worry about Will, my son, though. I know he's missing me."

"With luck it won't be too long."

"I hope not."

"Do take care, James. You're going into a very dangerous place."

"No more than thousands of soldiers have to endure. Although I did hear, Meg, that the end might really be in sight at last. Peace negotiations are underway, let's hope it's all over soon."

Meg didn't comment. However soon the end came, it looked like it hadn't been soon enough for David Falconer. She knew James must think the same but he didn't say as much.

They spoke a while longer, discussing practical matters, then Meg said good night and went to her room. She sat for a long while, her thoughts racing. So much had happened; it was hard to take it all in. She hoped fervently that the information James had received was correct, and that the young wounded officer was indeed his son. But even if it was David, and they brought him home safely, then there would be a whole new set of problems to face.

CHAPTER
SEVENTEEN

Jeannie Duncan gathered her things up in a bundle and crept quietly down the stairs, grimacing as the old wood creaked beneath her feet. She hated what she was doing, but she couldn't think of anything else. Running away was a cowardly thing to do, but she felt she had no option. Yes, she was letting people down — her mother, her family, Mrs Fraser, Will — but what other option did she have?

If she stayed she'd be sent back home to slave at the laundry work for her mother. No hope of getting to college, no hope of anything.

So she had decided to take matters into her own hands and escape from a world that was closing in on her. She crossed the yard, making for the barn where her old bike was kept.

It was just by chance that Will, wrestling with his geometry homework, happened to glance out of his bedroom window at that moment. He frowned as he saw the stealthy figure carrying a bundle. A burglar? Or Ina making a clandestine visit to her young man?

Then the moon came from behind a cloud and he recognized Jeannie as she slipped into the barn. A couple of minutes later she came out, pushing her bike, got on after a last look round and rode away out of the yard. Will waited no longer.

Quickly he scrambled into his thick jacket, trying to be as quiet as possible. He didn't want Miss Gillespie waking up and demanding to know what was going on. What was going on? Jeannie was running away, he was sure of it. He knew her mother would soon be out of hospital and putting two and two together he had guessed that Jeannie might be recalled home. And he knew for certain what her feelings on that score would be.

He hesitated a second. What right did he have to interfere? What good could it do? Perhaps he should let Jeannie ride away and do what she wanted with her life. He glanced back at his bed, warm and welcoming with its layers of blankets concealing a stone hot-water bottle filled from the kettle. Outside, the cold November night was wet and windy.

But he had to go. If anything happened to Jeannie, if she came to any harm, he'd never forgive himself. He thought about wakening Sandy — as Jeannie's brother he would feel he had a right to be consulted — but then he dismissed the thought. Sandy might well be too critical of his sister; he was capable of starting an argument and making things ten times worse. No, it would be better if Sandy knew nothing.

Quietly Will stole downstairs and out of the door. It wasn't locked; it never was. He hurried over to the barn and got his bike, cursing under his breath when he realized it had a flat tyre. As quickly as he could he pumped it up, but it was difficult in the dark and he lost valuable time.

Which way would Jeannie go? At the gate he peered down and just managed to make out tyre tracks in the mud, turning left, away from Aberdeen. She must have gone home. She'd only been carrying a small bundle; she probably wanted to pick up more things. He'd go and find her there and get her to talk to him.

The rain was pouring down now, beating into his face as he struggled along, and the wind threatened to knock him off his bike, but he persevered. At last he came to the run-down little cottage where Jeannie's family lived, and leaned his bike against a wall out of the wind. There was no sign of a light; he wondered if perhaps he'd been mistaken in supposing Jeannie would come here. But he might as well see if there was anybody in, then he could get some shelter. He knocked on the weatherbeaten door.

At first there was no answer, then Jeannie's voice hissed, "Who's there?"

"It's me. Will."

"What are you doing here? Go away and leave me alone!"

Will persisted. "For heaven's sake, Jeannie, I'm soaked to the skin. At least let me in to get dry by the fire. I'll catch my death if I go back in this."

The door swung open, and Jeannie stood there holding a candle. The wind caught it and blew it out, just as the moon went behind a cloud, leaving them in complete darkness.

"Now look what you've done!" Jeannie scolded. "Well, you might as well come in and help me find the matches."

They groped their way into the room, and after a bit of hunting Jeannie managed to get the candle relit. The small pool of light illuminated the two of them, but not much more.

"It's freezing in here!" Will exclaimed. "Nearly as cold as it is outside. The fire must have gone out."

"I've brought some sticks in," Jeannie said. "I'll get it going in a minute, then we can get the kettle on."

While she busied herself, Will found a couple more candles and lit them. The wavering light seemed to emphasize the gloominess of the small bare room. He shivered. "Where are the rest of the family? They should have banked the fire up to keep it in."

Jeannie, on her knees with her back to him as she coaxed the kindling into life, retorted, "The younger ones aren't here. They're staying with our neighbour down the road; they didn't like being on their own here at night. Which explains the lack of fire. And it also means that you and I are on our own here, so you shouldn't stay here any longer than you have to. You can imagine what people would say if they knew."

Will blushed scarlet. The thought hadn't occurred to him. Jeannie was so much more worldly-wise than he was.

"Well, if I go back I want you to come too," he challenged. "You're running away, aren't you? You can't do that; it's a cowardly way out."

202

At that Jeannie seemed to crumple. She stopped fanning at the fire and sat back on her heels. "You don't understand, do you? Well, look around you! Would you like to have to live like this?"

"But Jeannie, you have a duty to help your mother. Especially now when she's just coming out of hospital."

"Do you think I don't know that?" Jeannie flashed back. "Don't you see that when you're saying I should come back here you're looking at a short-term solution? *I'm* looking long term. Yes, I could stay here and lug washing about and help in that way. But I'd hate it, and I'm not even good at it. I'm useless at ironing, and I have no patience."

She picked up a couple of logs and threw them onto the small fire; they fizzed with damp. "But if I could just get away and train as a teacher, then I'd send money home to help the family. I'd be doing a useful, worthwhile job, one that I've always wanted to do. They're trying to stop me, so don't you see I absolutely have to go away!"

"But where would you go?" Will asked. "Have you thought it out?"

"Yes, I have," Jeannie said more calmly. "I'm going to Glasgow. I have an uncle there. I've saved enough money for the fare, and I'm going to get the early train."

"Does he know you're coming?"

"Well . . . no. He's my father's side of the family, and after Dad was killed Mum fell out with them. They haven't spoken since."

"Oh. So what makes you think he'd be glad to see you?"

Jeannie was silent, and Will went on, "I think you should come back with me, Jeannie. This is a half-baked idea of yours. When my mother comes back she'll know what to do."

"But I might be back here by then!" Jeannie cried despairingly.

"So? I'm sure Ma could still do something. She's very much in favour of helping people get on in life, and she's really got a bee in her bonnet about education. Why else do you think she makes me stay on at school? She might know someone who would take your place here while you go off to college. And if you come back then at least you could get in touch with your uncle and find out how he feels about it before you turn up on his doorstep. Don't you think it makes sense?"

"Well, maybe." Jeannie sighed. "Well, yes, you're right. I've just had a bad day; Ina was carping at me, and Miss Gillespie was criticizing the way I laid the table. I suppose I'd simply had enough. It all got too much for me."

"We all feel like that sometimes," Will said. "But look, Jeannie, if ever you feel like that you must talk to me about it. Promise? You're not on your own, you know."

Jeannie gave him a rueful smile. "You're very kind, Will. And very patient. I don't know what I can do to repay you."

204

Will stared at her for a long moment, then he shrugged and said, "You could always keep on giving me a hand with the schoolwork. There's a geometry problem I could use some help with."

For a moment he thought Jeannie had been expecting a different answer, but perhaps he was mistaken. She smiled again, as she said, "All right, you win. So, should we set off back right now, do you think?"

Will listened to the sound of the rain sluicing down the corrugated tin roof and the wind howling round the chimney. "Definitely not. We'd catch pneumonia. Let's have a cup of tea, if you can find any, then sit by the fire a bit to warm up before we go. We've got plenty of time before it gets light."

The tea in the caddy was mouldy, so they had to make do with hot water. Jeannie found a blanket that wasn't too damp, and they snuggled together for warmth in a battered old armchair in front of the fire. Will put an arm round Jeannie's shoulder and listened to her slow breathing as she fell asleep. He'd let her sleep for a while, he decided, then they had better set off back.

The next thing he knew a cockerel in the yard was crowing. He sat up abruptly and looked at his watch by the light of the dying fire.

"Oh no! It's after five! The horsemen will be up by now."

Jeannie struggled upright, rubbing her eyes. "Oh, Will, what shall we do?"

Will stood up. "We've got to go back and hope no one sees us. It's still dark, we should be all right. When we get to the farm I'll go first and check it's all clear. You can sneak into the house. Thank heaven Ina is a lazy thing. She won't be up yet. But we must hurry."

They rushed out to their bikes and pedalled furiously back to Braehead; Will was glad that it was downhill nearly all the way. Once there they stole along the back of the rick yard where they couldn't be seen from the stables.

"You go first," Will whispered. "If anyone comes along I'll hold them up."

"Thanks," Jeannie said. "And thanks for making me see sense." Before he realized what she was doing she'd stood on tiptoe and briefly kissed his cheek. Then she was gone, hurrying across the yard to the house. Will waited a while, then he sauntered across the yard as though he had every reason to be there. He went round to the front and in that way, congratulating himself that they had got away with it.

What he didn't realize was that Ina's dread of Miss Gillespie's caustic tongue had got her out of bed good and early for once. She was standing in the shadows just inside the kitchen door, and saw him come in, his coat dripping wet. She raised her eyebrows and smiled to herself as she drew back out of sight.

"He's in here, sir." The medical orderly led the way along a drab narrow corridor to a door at the end. "He's had a good night and he's expecting you."

"Thank you." James knocked at the door, trying to prepare himself for what he might find inside. Would his son recognize him?

"Come in."

Instantly James felt a rush of emotion; that was unmistakably David's voice. He went into the room, his heart thumping.

"David! Son, it's good to see you!" He almost ran over to the bed where his son lay propped up against the pillows. David looked frail and drawn; there was a long scar over his left temple, and a cradle supported the blankets above his legs. But he held out a hand to his father, and his grip was firmer than James would have expected.

For a moment neither could speak, then at last James said gruffly, "We'd just about given up on you, son. I can't tell you what this means to me."

"Sorry for causing so much trouble!" David grinned at him with a flash of his old humour. "I'll have to be more careful in future."

"Let's hope your future will be somewhere else. They say that this show might be over soon enough. Either way I'm taking you back with me; that is, if you're well enough to travel."

"I'm well enough." There was determination in David's voice which his father remembered of old. "But never mind all that. Have you news of Isobel? Where is she?"

James had worried about how much to tell David, but faced with the look in his son's eyes he knew he would have to tell him everything. "She's at our house in Kent."

"What? Why? Is she on leave?"

"She's not been well — she had a dose of influenza." James explained briefly, trying to make light of Isobel's illness so as not to worry David unduly. "But I'm glad to say she's on the mend."

"Does she know about — about all this?"

"No. We thought it better not to tell her. At the time they weren't entirely certain who you were —"

David laughed. "Well, I'm one hundred per cent certain who I am! And you can speak up for me, Pa." His expression became more serious. "But I'm glad no one's told her, because I want to do it myself. When I walk in through the door."

James frowned. "But, son, the extent of your injuries . . . They warned us you'd be in a wheelchair for a good long time. That you might not —"

He broke off, not wanting to say the words. David had to finish the sentence for him. "Might not ever walk again? Oh, I know. They've said it to me. What rot! They don't know what they're talking about."

"No? From what I heard you're lucky still to have your legs."

"Surely. The surgeon did a magnificent job. And I'm carrying around a significant amount of German government property, you know. There are still lots of bits of shrapnel in there that ain't going to come out, and yes, one of my legs will always be shorter than the other one so I'll walk with a limp. But, dammit, I *will* walk!"

James's expression must have given away his thoughts, for David said angrily, "All right then, I'll show you! Just reach under the mattress for me, will you?"

Surprised, James did as he asked and pulled out a pair of crutches. "Where did these come from?"

"Ah, one of the nurses smuggled them in for me. The old charm is still working, you see. Now watch this."

Before James could try to stop him, David had pushed back the blankets and with some difficulty, swung his legs out of bed. James winced at the sight of the frail limbs swathed in army-issue pyjamas, and at the way David bit down on his lower lip to cope with the pain.

He took the crutches from his father, set them under his arms, and with a considerable effort struggled to his feet. "There! How's that? I've been practising, you see, late at night when the medicos aren't around to stop me. Susie has been my partner in crime; I owe her a decent present when I get out of here. She's been terrific. Now let's see . . ."

Stiffly, agonizingly, he took a tentative step. James, watching felt his eyes fill with tears, but he blinked them back. It was torture for him to watch his once-athletic son struggling to put one foot in front of the other. Every instinct urged him to go and help, but he knew David would not want it.

"That's pretty good!" he said at last. "But don't you think you've done enough for one day?"

"Oh, I don't know about that. I try to do a bit more each day. How about a grand tour —"

And then to James's horror one of the crutches skidded on the wooden floor, David lost his balance and crashed to the ground. For a moment he lay there while James sat shocked into immobility, then he started to struggle to his feet.

"David, let me —"

"I don't — need — any help." David spoke through gritted teeth. Slowly he reached up and got hold of the bed frame and laboriously, breathing hard, he heaved himself up onto the bed. Once there he closed his eyes. James, deperately afraid that the young man would lose consciousness, went over to his side. "Come on, you've made your point. Let's get you back into bed before Matron comes and gives us both a ticking off."

David, chalk white, allowed his father to help him back in and to rearrange the blankets. Then he lay back and managed a grin. "See? I'm serious about this, you know."

"I know." James voice was choked. "And son, I'm with you all the way. Whatever you need to get you walking again, you shall have it."

He turned away, not wanting David to see how emotional he felt. He was going to do everything in his power to help his son to walk again, but he knew it would be a long, hard struggle and the final outcome was far from certain.

·

CHAPTER
EIGHTEEN

"Another letter from your mother, young Will." Mr Greig, the postie, held out the bundle to Will. "I hope she'll soon be back with you, bringing that sister of yours. It can't be a day too soon."

"You're right there. We all miss her." Will took the letters. "You'll come in for a fly cup? It's a nasty cold morning."

The postie shook his head. "Thanks, lad, but I must be getting on. I've a heavy load to get through today. But you'll have heard the news?"

"What news?"

Mr Greig pursed his lips. "A bad business, aye, a bad business, though there's those who would have said he had it coming to him."

"Who? What?" Will knew the postie liked to spin out his news in order to get maximum effect from it, but right at that moment he didn't have time to stand and listen.

"Why, Dod Grant, of course." Mr Greig looked mildly affronted that Will was being so impatient. "The poor man's been found dead." Anticipating Will's next question, he went on dramatically. "Murdered!"

"What!" Will stared in shock. "How did it happen? Where was he?"

"He was found early this morning, but they think it happened a few days ago. The last time he was seen alive was at the inn on Friday night. He'd been hit over the head — a terrible business. What's the world coming to when honest people can't sleep easy in their beds?"

"But who —"

"That's the question, isn't it?" Mr Greig looked pleased that Will was taking an interest at last. "Old Miss McKenzie, his housekeeper, was away visiting her sister, so he was all alone in the house. Someone after his money, I've no doubt. They do say he has a whole heap of it stashed away somewhere, though you'd never think it to look at him. Maybe they found it, the blackguards."

A voice came from behind them. "Good morning, Mr Greig. I hope you're not letting Master Will keep you back." The angular form of Miss Gillespie came into view, and the postie hastily got back on his bike.

"And good morning to you too, Miss Gillespie. I'll be on my way now. I'll leave young Will to give you the terrible news. Ach, terrible it is."

Shaking his head he rode off down the brae, leaving Will to tell Miss Gillespie about Dod Grant's demise. She was suitably shocked.

"Why, the poor man! He wasn't well liked, of course, but one wouldn't wish this on anyone. What a mercy for poor Annie that she was away, or she might have suffered the same fate too. What will become of her, I wonder? And the funeral, so difficult for my father in this cold weather. Standing around in the kirkyard is so bad for his rheumatics. And I expect the police will be round making enquiries. Not that there's much we can tell them, I don't suppose."

"No."

Will put the matter out of his mind as best he could while he read his mother's letter. What he read there was of far greater significance, and he lost no time in telling Jeannie when he found her cleaning the parlour fireplace.

"Isobel's fiancé is alive, after all, would you believe it? Only he's been badly wounded — well, not that badly, I suppose. Ma didn't say exactly, but he's on the mend. And Isobel's not to know about it yet on account of her having been so ill. She'll be amazed I should think. And I daresay they'll both come up here and there'll be a wedding in the family. I've never been to a wedding, do you know that?"

"I hope you enjoy it." There was a flatness in Jeannie's voice that brought Will out of his euphoria.

"Hey, is old Miss Gillespie working you too hard? She's a tartar that one, but it'll be fine when Ma comes home —"

"No, it's not that." Jeannie got to her feet. "It's Ina."

"Ina? What's she been up to?" Will spoke confidently, but inwardly he was anxious. Ina usually spelled trouble.

"Oh, nothing really. She just keeps going around looking at me strangely — with a sort of smirk. And she makes odd remarks like "gey cold weather to be out late" and things like that. Oh, Will, you don't think she knows, do you?"

"I'm sure she doesn't," Will said, trying to believe it. "Anyway, if she did know anything she'd have been on to me about it before now. No, she's probably just winding you up, that's all."

"I hope so."

"I'm sure so. Now, have you heard the news about Dod Grant?" Will changed the subject quickly to distract Jeannie from her worries. He was halfway through his account when Miss Gillespie came into the room.

"Now, Jeannie, don't stand there chatting to Master Will, get on with your duties. You'll make him late for school."

When Will returned home late that afternoon he noticed an air of excitement around the farm. Rather than being about their work, the farmhands were standing about in small groups talking in low voices. They looked up as he approached and gave him their usual greeting, but there was a strange mood about them, as though they knew something he didn't, and they weren't going to tell him.

Miss Gillespie met him at the door. She too seemed affected by it; she seemed very much on edge.

"There are two policemen here, Will, wanting to speak to you. It's about that awful business with poor Mr Grant. A routine call, and I doubt that you will be able to tell them anything. They've already spoken to the men. You didn't see Jeannie Duncan on the bus, did you? It's her afternoon off and I think she went into town. The police will be wanting to speak to her too, and Ina."

"No, she wasn't on it," Will said. "She'll probably be getting a lift from the carter."

"Good, good. But you'd better not keep them waiting. Come along."

Will followed her through to the front parlour where a policeman in uniform and a plain-clothes officer sat gingerly on the horsehair-stuffed sofa. They stood up when he went in.

"Ah, Master Fraser," the detective said. "Would you take a seat, please?"

Miss Gillespie went out, and the man went on, "We're seeking information about a murder that has taken place at Overton Farm. The deceased is Mr George Grant. You know him?"

"Why . . . yes." Will hesitated slightly, unaccustomed to hearing Dod Grant's proper name.

"You knew him well?"

"Not really. I mean, he's a bit older than me, isn't he? I tend to choose friends of my own age."

The policeman taking notes looked up sharply at this, and the detective frowned. It occurred to Will that his attempts to be light-hearted were rather out of place, so he sat in silence, waiting for the next question. When it came, it took him by surprise.

"Mr Grant was last seen three days ago. Earlier that day several witnesses saw you having an altercation with Mr Grant. Would you like to tell us about it, please?"

Will stiffened. "I — well, I —"

"Yes?"

"Well, he made some remarks about my mother that I found offensive, so —"

"So you knocked him to the ground?"

"No! He backed into his horse and it reared."

"He backed into the horse when you threatened him?"

"No! Or, well, maybe. Possibly." Will thought for a moment. "But Dr Jim was there. He'll tell you what happened."

"We've already interviewed Dr Nicol," the detective said, "and he admitted that he had not seen what happened."

"Ah."

The questioner changed tack. "I believe there was a dispute between your family and Mr Grant. One of the farm workers, Alexander Duncan —"

"Who? Oh, you mean Sandy."

"*Alexander* Duncan," the detective went on, "said he overheard Mrs Fraser and Mr Grant having an argument. He was cutting grass outside the window."

Will felt his temper rising. "You'd better ask my mother herself about that," he retorted, "and if you're trying to pin this on her you'll not get very far because she's been in Kent for over a week now."

The two policemen exchanged glances. "We have no intention on pinning anything, as you put it, on your mother, but we certainly will wish to speak to her at some point. But perhaps the dispute might have coloured your attitude towards Mr Grant."

216

"Possibly," Will admitted. It seemed pointless to state otherwise.

There was a pause, broken only by the sound of scribbling, then the detective asked, "Master Fraser, could you tell us, please, where you were on Friday night?"

Will swallowed hard. Friday night. He had gone after Jeannie, had stayed in the deserted cottage with her all night when they both fell asleep. But he couldn't possibly admit that. "Why, I was here of course."

"All night?"

Will hesitated. "Er . . ."

"Think carefully, please."

There was a short silence; Will's mind raced. It sounded as if they suspected something, *knew* something. But he knew they hadn't spoken to Jeannie yet. Sandy knew nothing, he was sure. Surely, Ina . . . ? Might she have seen him go out? Or come back in? One thing was clear. He couldn't betray Jeannie, if it became known that they had been together all night her reputation would be ruined. Her teaching career would be over before it had begun. He had to say something though, but what?

He cleared his throat. "All right, yes, I was out on Friday night."

"May I ask where?"

"I — I was with a friend."

"And that friend would back up your statement?"

"I — I'd rather they were not involved."

"I see." The two men exchanged glances. Will felt trapped. He could feel a trickle of sweat running down from his brow. If only his mother were here!

"Very well, Master Fraser." The older man got to his feet. "I'm afraid I'm going to have to ask you to come down to the station with us. To help us with our enquiries."

Will ran his tongue over his suddenly dry lips. "Certainly. I'd be happy to help. But first — may I have a moment to tell Miss Gillespie what's happening?"

He managed to keep his voice under control, but inwardly he was desperately afraid. It was a relief when the detective nodded, and Will almost ran out of the room. But he didn't go to the kitchen where he knew Miss Gillespie would be sitting with Ina, he hurried out into the yard in search of Sandy.

He found him in the stable, cleaning harness. There was no one else there.

"Sandy!"

"Will, what is it? Have the bobbies been speaking to you? What —"

"There's no time for that now." Will spoke urgently, with a backwards look over his shoulder. Any moment, he feared, the two men might come looking for him. "They're taking me in for questioning —"

"What!"

"It'll be all right. But you must give a message to Jeannie. Tell her I said nothing about Friday and she mustn't either. Understand? She'll know what I mean. It's desperately important."

Sandy narrowed his eyes. "What's going on here?" he asked dangerously.

"Nothing. I promise. Look, they mustn't see me talking to you. I have to go. Remember to tell Jeannie."

With that, Will turned and ran back to the house. Had he done enough to protect Jeannie?

CHAPTER
NINETEEN

Meg looked anxiously around the crowded platform of the Aberdeen railway station. Was everyone staring at her, she wondered, or was it just her imagination? People must surely know by now that her son was being held by the police, arrested on suspicion of murder.

She'd been unable to sleep on the long journey north, in a fever of impatience to get back home and sort everything out. There must be some mistake; there had to be. She was certain that once everyone sat down calmly and went through all the facts, they would realize that Will could not possibly be guilty of such an appalling crime. But in the meantime the poor lad must be going through hell.

As she was herself, if she was honest. If only she'd been able to share the terrible news with someone before she set off for home. But James had been away in France on his mission to fetch his wounded son back home, and of course there was no question of letting Isobel know anything about her young brother's plight. She was scarcely over her dangerous illness, and in no fit state to cope with upsetting news.

Isobel didn't even know that David had been found. Meg and James had decided that they would wait to see what sort of condition he was in before they said anything to his fiancée. And that was another worry — but Meg resolutely pushed it from her mind. There was nothing she could do about that, whereas she was going to need all her mental strength to deal with Will and his problems.

"Mistress Fraser!"

Meg glanced over in the direction of the voice, and smiled as she recognized Alec, the farm foreman, who had been in charge during her absence.

"It's good to see you, Alec. Where's the trap?"

"It's waiting outside, mistress. Let me take that."

He picked up her heavy bag and set off out of the station with Meg following behind. She sensed that he wanted to get her away from prying eyes. Once they were on the road they would have privacy to talk.

It was only as they left the city behind that Meg dared broach the subject of Will. "Please tell me what's been happening, Alec," she asked. "I've heard the bare details from the police down in Kent. They came to speak to me, but of course I wasn't able to help them at all. I was down there when poor Dod Grant was murdered. I can't imagine why they think Will had anything to do with it."

"They'll have told you he was out at the time it happened?" Alec said. "That he was unable, or unwilling, to tell them where he was?"

"I did hear that, yes, but, heavens, it must have just slipped his memory. He probably got flustered. Surely he's remembered by now?"

221

"No, mistress, he has not. Or, I should say, he is not willing to tell them anything. He was out of the house all night, no one knows where. You can see how that looks bad for him. Especially as he'd been seen earlier on having a big argument with Mr Grant — knocked the fellow over, they say." Meg said nothing, and Alec went on, "I know Dod Grant had few friends, but no one hated him enough to do away with him. In any case, those who have had disagreements with him recently all have alibis for the night he was killed. Except Master Will."

"And the police will know that we at Braehead were having a dispute with Dod about the water," Meg said slowly. "But surely they can see that murder is no sort of solution!"

"Of course it isn't, but their way of thinking seems to be that young Master Will went over there to try and reason with him. When Dod refused to budge the lad lost his temper and went for him."

"With what?"

"They don't know. No sort of weapon has been found, and your son isn't saying anything. Just denying the fact that he was there."

"So who says he was out of the house?"

"Ina. Says she saw him coming back in very early in the morning, soaked to the skin and looking very guilty-like. And he's admitted he was out, just refuses to say where or why."

Meg's lips thinned. She intended to have words with Ina. But first of all she desperately wanted to talk to her son. There had to be some simple answer to all of this.

He must be persuaded to tell the police where he was that night, then everything would be all right — surely?

Isobel couldn't concentrate on the book she was reading. She threw it down, got up from the table and paced over to the window, looking down into the rain-soaked garden.

She wished she could go out into town, perhaps do some shopping — anything! She felt so much better in herself, able to cope with anything now, and she was bored.

It had been bad enough when Mr Falconer had had to go away so suddenly on business, but then yesterday her mother had suddenly left too, saying only that something on the farm urgently needed her attention. Isobel had pleaded to be allowed to go too, but her mother had been adamant.

Which had left Isobel on her own most of the day. The housekeeper popped in for a chat now and then, and there was the doctor's daily visit, but other than that the time passed slowly.

Just then Isobel noticed a motor car drawing up outside. She recognized it as Mr Falconer's car; he had promised her a ride in it once she was feeling better. She looked out with interest. That must mean that he was back from his business trip, and she would have company for dinner once again.

There seemed to be someone else in the car. Isobel noticed the housekeeper and one of the maids scurrying outside, and then the doctor's car drew up behind. She felt a stab of anxiety. Could Mr Falconer have been taken ill? Or her mother?

She began to feel that her curiosity was out of place, so she came away from the window and sat down again with her book, but it totally failed to engage her attention. Her ears were straining to pick up any sound that might give some clue to what was happening downstairs.

A door banged; she heard voices and footsteps in the tiled hall. Then silence.

Just as she felt she could bear it no longer and she would have to leave her room to find out for herself what was going on, there was a knock at her door.

"Come in!" Her voice was unsteady, but she forced herself to keep calm.

The door opened and James Falconer came in. He looked tired, Isobel noted, and uncharacteristically uncertain.

"Isobel, how are you feeling today? I was so sorry to hear that your mother had had to go home. Did she say anything to you about the reason?"

"I'm feeling much better, thanks. And no, she didn't say why she had to leave. Well — just something about the farm." A sudden doubt struck her. "There's nothing terribly wrong, is there? There hasn't been some sort of accident? Will — is Will all right, do you know?"

"He's fine." James walked over to the fireplace and held out his hands to the warmth. What he had said was true enough in one respect, he told himself; Will was in good health, as far as he knew. But he had just read the note Meg had left for him, briefly telling him that Will

224

was a murder suspect, and not to let Isobel know anything about it. He was still reeling from the news, and it was so difficult not to give anything away.

"No, I understand it's some problem on the farm," he said, keeping his back to Isobel so that she wouldn't see his expression. "I'm sure it's nothing your mother can't sort out."

He spoke with more conviction there. Surely the whole affair must be some ghastly misunderstanding, and once Meg was home she would put everything to rights in her usual capable way. He couldn't allow himself to worry about it, because there was something else — *someone* else — claiming his attention.

He came to a swift decision. He would tell Isobel that David was back. He had been wondering whether to keep the news from her until David had recovered from the long and difficult journey, but no, it was best to tell her straight away. It would not do to let her find out by accident, and her concern for David would stop her worrying about her mother and brother.

He came over and sat beside her, taking her hands in his.

"Isobel, dear, I've got some very, very good news."

She stared at him for a moment, then her eyes filled with tears. "It's David, isn't it —"

"Yes. He's alive. That's why I went away. I went over to France to bring him back."

Isobel had jumped to her feet. "Alive? He's alive? Then where is he? I must go to him! Why isn't he here to see me?"

James got to his feet. "Not so fast, sweetheart. He's been wounded — no, don't worry, he's over the worst and well on the road to recovery — but the journey tired him out. The doctor's given him something and he's sleeping now. You'll have to be patient just a little while longer."

Isobel buried her face in her hands. "I can't believe this. Why did no one tell me before?"

"I'm sorry. We were acting for the best as we thought, with you having been so ill. The thing was, at first we weren't sure whether it really was David. He'd lost his memory. Let me explain."

He patted the sofa beside him and Isobel sat down again, her eyes never leaving his face as he told her about how David had been found after such a long time.

"And how is he?" she asked urgently. "You say he's wounded? Where exactly?"

Seeing him hesitate she added, "Don't forget I was a VAD. I've nursed scores of wounded men. I can cope, whatever it is."

"It's his legs," James said quietly. "It was very bad, but the doctors managed to save them. He's in a wheelchair —"

He was going to say "and he might never walk again" but something stopped him. He remembered David's fierce determination to get back on his feet. Would that ever happen? He didn't know.

"So when can I see him?" Isobel asked tremulously. "Do I have to wait until tomorrow? Is that what you're saying?"

226

James started to speak but she interrupted him.

"I don't mind. Really I don't. In fact it's probably a good thing, it gives me time to get used to the idea I'm really going to see him again. I can hardly believe it's true. All this time we all thought he was dead. I just have to convince myself that he's not —"

And then the tears she'd been holding back welled up and spilled down her cheeks. All the pent-up emotion couldn't be restrained any longer. James took her in his arms and stroked her hair, blinking back tears himself.

"It's all right, Isobel, you have a good cry. You'll feel better for it. You and David are going to have so much to say to each other tomorrow morning."

CHAPTER
TWENTY

Meg sat at one side of the bare wooden table facing her son. The pale light of the autumn morning filtered into the room through the barred window.

"Will, I can't understand why you're holding back," she urged. "If you would only tell the police where you were that night, then all this could be cleared up."

Will shook his head. "I can't."

Meg made another attempt. "I don't think you realize how serious things are. Don't you realize that you are the number one murder suspect —"

"I didn't do it, and they can't prove I did! Innocent until proven guilty, that's how the law works, isn't it? Well, let them try!"

"But they are trying, and if we're not careful they may succeed in bringing a charge. They say they already have a motive —"

"Of sorts!"

"A capable lawyer could make a great deal of that. You were seen to assault Mr Grant, and everyone knows we had a grievance against him." She took a deep breath, willing herself to have patience. "Look, son, you could put an end to all this simply by telling us where you were that night. Is there anyone who could testify on your behalf?"

"No."

Will's mouth was set in a firm line, and Meg knew she was getting nowhere with him. He had inherited her own strength of will, and she realized that once he had made his mind up nothing was going to change it.

He must be protecting someone, she thought. A bit of poaching, perhaps? Some prank that went wrong?

She decided she would have a word with some of his friends, see if they could shed any light on the matter. Yes, they had probably been questioned already, but if she could only make them see the gravity of the situation then she hoped they would be more forthcoming. First she was going to see the solicitor and find out what he had to say.

Later she bumped into Ellen Nicol.

"Meg! How wonderful to see you back! How's Isobel?"

Meg, depressed at hearing the solicitor's pessimistic opinion, had to work hard to dredge up a smile. "She's doing very well, thanks. By now she'll have had the best tonic of all — her fiancé is alive after all and his father was going to break the news to her. The two of them might even have met again by now."

"That's incredible! Doesn't it do you good, to hear a bit of good news for a change? But, Meg, Jim and I were so distressed to hear about Will being held on suspicion of that awful business with Dod Grant. I hope he's home by now?"

"No, he isn't, but I hope it won't be long. I've asked the solicitor to see what he can do."

"Well, if there's any way we can help, do say. Jim feels personally responsible, you know."

"What? How?"

"Because he couldn't truthfully say he saw what happened when Dod Grant got knocked over. They say Will assaulted him; Jim was sure he didn't, but he couldn't swear to it."

Meg sighed. "Tell him not to worry, Ellen. I don't think it would make a lot of difference either way. No, the boy is his own worst enemy. He's still refusing to say where he was on the night it happened."

"Do you think he's shielding someone?"

"It's beginning to look like that. And the trouble is, he doesn't realize what danger he's putting himself in. He probably thinks he's being very loyal, but he's just being stupid. I only hope he realizes before it's too late."

"Surely they won't charge him formally?"

"I really don't know. The solicitor says it could come to that if they feel they have a case. And it's all so unnecessary. All he has to do is prove he wasn't there."

Unless, Meg suddenly thought, with a chill of apprehension, unless he was there. So far she hadn't allowed herself to think like that, but perhaps she was going to have to face the possibility that her son had indeed committed the crime.

She excused herself from Ellen and walked off along the street, not really caring where she was going. She just needed time to think.

230

She saw a figure she recognized and forced herself to smile. "Hello, Jeannie. Enjoying your afternoon off?"

Jeannie looked flustered. "Oh. Mrs Fraser, yes, I — that is, yes, I'm in town with my brother. We're looking for a present for Mum. It's her birthday this weekend."

"I see. Well, remind me to send her something — a nice joint of pork perhaps. She needs to keep her strength up."

"Thank you, ma'am, that's very kind of you."

Jeannie watched Meg walk away. She felt very uneasy. She could see that Mrs Fraser looked distraught, even though on the surface she was her usual calm self. She must be so worried about her son, and Jeannie knew that one word from herself to the police and Will would be in the clear. But he'd made her promise to say nothing, and now that promise was hanging very heavily on her.

She saw her brother coming towards her, and decided she simply had to confide in him.

"All right, Sis?" he greeted her. "What's up? You look like the world's away to end tomorrow."

"That's a bit how it feels," Jeannie responded flatly.

"Worried about Will? There's no need to be, you know. There's bound to be someone who can vouch for him."

"That's just it. Suppose that person was me?"

Sandy's eyes narrowed. "What do you mean?"

"We can't talk here, in the middle of the street. Let's go down to the harbour."

Not waiting to see if he was following, she set off down towards the sea. There, leaning on the wall, she told him how she and Will had spent the night in the deserted cottage.

Sandy heard her out in silence, his expression thunderous. "I don't believe this!" he exclaimed when she'd finished. "You were there all night, just the two of you?"

"Yes, but I've told you, nothing happened. We just fell asleep —"

"And who's going to believe that!"

Jeannie's anger ignited to match his. "You, for a start! At least I hope so. Or do you think your sister's a —"

"Of course I don't! I know you better than that. But no one else will believe you." Jeannie said nothing, so he went on, "And this would be the end of any thoughts you might have had about a teaching career. They'd never take you on if this comes out."

"I know that," Jeannie said quietly, "but I have to tell the truth to the police. I have to put the record straight."

"But what about our mother? Have you thought about her?"

"What do you mean?" Jeannie's throat was suddenly dry.

"Well, you know these respectable ladies who employ her to do their washing? They aren't going to want to do business with a disgraced family, are they? They'll take their custom elsewhere — just as Mum's getting back on her feet with Molly McKenzie to help her. And I shouldn't think Molly's father will let her keep on working for us; he's an elder of the kirk and has his position to think of. And," Sandy continued relentlessly, "what about the effect on Mum herself? She's only just getting over a serious operation; news like this could have her right back in hospital. You can't do this to her, Jeannie."

Jeannie was close to tears. She felt completely hopeless. "But what about Will? He could be charged with a crime he didn't commit."

"They can't prove anything. They'll have to let him go sooner or later."

"I wish I could believe that." Jeannie wasn't convinced. She turned to face her brother, the wind whipping her hair back from her face. "I'll give it one more day. If they're still holding Will by that time I'll go and tell them everything. I don't care what happens."

Isobel sat on the sofa, trying to be composed. She glanced down at her hands, clasped in her lap, and took a deep breath. She had to appear calm for David's sake, but inwardly she was a jangle of nerves. Exactly what state would she find him in? How bad were his injuries? How would they cope?

But one thing above all, she longed to feel his arms around her again, hear him whisper her name. Nothing else was important.

She heard voices outside the door. Anxiously she rose to her feet. The door opened, and there was her fiancé, sitting in a wheelchair, pushed by his father.

"David!" She took a couple of steps forward, and then stopped at the sight of his face. It was set and cold. She tried again. "Oh, David, it's so wonderful to see you, we've got so much to talk about." Her voice trailed away and she cast an appealing glance at his father. This wasn't how she'd expected things!

He cleared his throat. "Well, perhaps I'll leave you two together for a while. Not too long though — we don't want to tire Isobel out."

With an attempt at a smile, he went out and left them. Silence yawned.

Isobel broke it. "I can't believe this is happening. I've prayed for this moment —"

She tried to take his hand, but David pulled it away. "This moment?" he echoed bitterly. "When you see me being trundled about like a baby in a pushchair? Is this really what you expected?"

"David, I —"

"I wanted you to see me on my feet, walking. I tried so hard but I couldn't manage it. What use am I to anyone like this?"

"You mustn't think like this," Isobel said desperately. "I don't care about the wheelchair. I thought I was never going to see you ever again, and now this is like a miracle."

"A miracle? This?" David slumped back in the chair. "What sort of a husband would I make? No, I've been thinking hard about things, and I've decided to release you from our engagement."

His words shocked Isobel to the core, but she pulled herself together. Anger flared in her. He was being self-pitying, completely selfish! He couldn't see beyond his own problems. This wasn't the David Falconer she

234

had fallen in love with, and she had to make him snap out of this despairing mood.

"Oh, you have, have you?" she challenged. "You've decided that? You didn't think to consult me first?"

"What is there to consult about? You can see how things are."

Isobel sensed his despair and her heart went out to him. She knelt on the floor beside his chair, grasping his hand and holding it tight.

"Yes, I can see how things are, and it makes absolutely no difference to the way I feel. I love you, David Falconer, and I'm just as determined as I ever was to be your wife. And I'm certainly not releasing you from our engagement. Do you want to be had up for breach of promise?"

David turned to her, his eyes wide in disbelief. "Do you really mean that? You still want to marry me, even like this?"

"Try and stop me. And what do you mean, 'like this'? Your father's been telling me how determined you are to get back on your feet. You're not going to be in that wheelchair for ever."

He shook his head. "I tried again this morning, but my wretched legs just gave way."

"That's not surprising, is it? You've just had a very hard journey; you must be exhausted. And these things take time. As a doctor you must know that."

He gave her a grudging nod. "All right, Nurse. But it's not just the legs, bad though they are. Any sort of sudden noise sets my nerves on edge — a car backfiring, even the traffic in the streets. It awakens bad memories, makes me feel like a nervous wreck."

"You'll get over it, I know you will," Isobel urged. She was fighting for their future, she knew; she simply had to get David out of this black mood. "If we could get you away from the city for a while you'd be fine."

"Where to? There's a war on, you know."

"I know!" Isobel jumped to her feet. "I'll take you to Scotland, to my home at Braehead. Remember how we used to talk about going there? You'll meet my mother, my brother Will, oh, and Dr Jim Nicol — he's a real character! And it's so peaceful up there, it will do you the world of good!"

Her brow clouded for a moment as she remembered how her mother had left suddenly because of some problem on the farm, but she pushed the thought to the back of her mind. There were always minor problems cropping up on the farm, and her mother always dealt with them calmly and efficiently. By the time they got David up there everything would be back to normal, she was sure of it.

"We'll have to take the journey in stages," she said, half to herself. "That will be like a holiday in itself. We'll have you back on your feet, I know we will."

"Let me try now." David flung back the tartan rug that covered his knees.

"David, are you sure —" Isobel moved forward anxiously, then checked herself. He had to be allowed to try.

Slowly, painfully, David levered himself upright. He grabbed hold of a chair back and took a single step away from the wheelchair. Then, for the first time, he smiled. "Well, that's a start."

Isobel's eyes were full of tears. She went over to him and put her arms gently round his waist. "The start of a long journey," she said softly. "I love you, Captain Falconer, and don't you forget it."

They didn't notice the door open and James Falconer walk in. He stood still for a moment, not wanting to break the spell, and half afraid that a sudden movement would unsettle David and make him lose his balance.

At last they noticed him. "See, Dad?" David said with a grin. "I made it after all."

"So you did, son," James said gruffly. "Now let's see if we can get you back into the chair."

With a bit of help David managed it, and the three of them sat down together, while Isobel outlined her plan for taking David up to Scotland. "Don't you think it's a good idea?" she appealed to James.

"Well —" James hesitated. Yes, Braehead would be an ideal place for his son to convalesce, but he knew all too well what problems Meg was facing. Would she be able to sort them out in time for Isobel and David to come and stay?

CHAPTER
TWENTY-ONE

Jeannie stood on the pavement outside the police station and took a deep breath as she glanced up at the forbidding exterior. In a few short minutes, she realized, she was going to ruin her whole life. And not only hers; things could never be the same for her mother, her brother Sandy, or any of their family, not once the police had heard what she had to say. And she'd be breaking her promise to Will. He'd probably never speak to her again.

But she simply had to do it. She had to tell the truth about what happened that night. It was the only way to prove that Will was innocent. So after a quick look to check there was no one she knew within sight, she pushed open the heavy door and went in. Once inside she went up to the first police officer she saw, an elderly sergeant at the desk, who looked as if he might be understanding.

"Excuse me," she said timidly.

"What is it, lassie?" The man's voice was kind. "Not been and lost your purse, I hope? The number of young lasses who can't look after their belongings —" He stopped as he took in Jeannie's pale set face and obvious distress. No, this was something different.

238

"I — I've come to give you some information," Jeannie blurted out. "About a crime. I — I'm a witness, or, well, not exactly. I can prove somebody didn't do it."

She was close to tears, and the sergeant could see it. "Wait there a minute, miss. Don't you go away now."

He left the desk, then a couple of minutes later he was back with a younger constable. "Right. Constable Watt is going to take over here while you and I go into this room here for a wee chat. Would you like a cup of tea?"

"No, thank you," Jeannie managed. He was being so kind. But she was sure his manner would change when he heard what she had to say. She followed him into a room heated by a pot-bellied stove and sat down on a wooden chair by a table. The sergeant sat opposite.

"Now, suppose I ask you just a few questions first. Take your time. First of all, we need to know what the crime is you want to tell us about."

Jeannie bit her lip. This was the moment of no return. She had to go ahead now. "It's to do with the murder of Mr Dod Grant," she said.

The sergeant looked up from his notepad in surprise. He had assumed that Jeannie would want to talk about some petty crime, but her admission had put things on a completely different level. By rights he knew he should get one of the more senior officers in to deal with this, but something stopped him.

"I see. And may I have your name, miss?"

Jeannie gave it.

"And address?"

She hesitated. "Well, I suppose . . . Braehead Farm —"

"Ah. And that's where the young lad is from who's helping us with our enquiries. Are you a friend of the family perhaps?"

"No. I'm one of the maids."

"And what exactly have you to tell me, my dear?"

Jeannie stared down at the table top, not wanting to meet his gaze. "I can prove that Will didn't do it. I can tell you where he was on the night the crime was committed. He was with me. All night."

By the silence that followed she knew she had shocked the policeman. She rushed on, "It wasn't like you think. I was running away; he came after me. We both fell asleep — Oh, what's the point, no one is going to believe me. But I don't care. Will was with me, and I'll swear to that, and I don't care what anyone thinks."

"Steady on, lassie," the sergeant interrupted her. He was sympathetic — he had a daughter of about Jeannie's age, and he could see what she must be going through. But this was not something he could deal with himself. "I'll have to get one of the officers working on this case to come and speak to you," he said, as kindly as he could. "He's got someone in for questioning about something else at the moment, but I'll see if he can spare some time to talk to you. He'll take down what you have to say. You just tell him what you told me, and —" He was going to say "everything will be all right" but he knew it wouldn't. It had taken courage for Jeannie to tell her story, and he could guess all too well what the consequences would be.

240

When he had gone Jeannie sat in dismal silence. Well, then, she had done it. Will should be safe now, or he certainly would be after she had spoken to the next police officer. Then what would happen? Shame and disgrace. Perhaps the whole family would have to leave the area and start afresh. How would her mother react? Maybe she'll cast me off, Jeannie thought miserably. And what would Mrs Fraser say?

Her depressing thoughts were interrupted by the return of the police sergeant. To her surprise he carried a cup of tea and a plate of biscuits on a tray. More surprising still, he was smiling.

He put the tray on the table and sat down. "I have some good news for you, lassie. Looks like your story's not going to be needed after all."

Jeannie stared at him, speechless with shock, as he went on. "Late last night they picked up a vagrant, suspected of housebreaking. He's being questioned right now. Anyway, it seems he had some of Dod Grant's possessions on him, and not only that, he was carrying what looks like it might be the murder weapon. He's admitted he did it, though he claims it was an accident. Mr Grant discovered him breaking into the house and there was a scuffle; I don't really know the details. But that means young Will Fraser's in the clear, and they've already sent up to Braehead for his folks to come and take him home. They'll be here any moment; you could get a lift back if you like."

After a moment's stunned silence, Jeannie burst into tears. She could hardly believe what she'd just heard. "So I didn't need — I could have said nothing —"

She was appalled at what she'd done. Now her guilty secret was out in the open and all for nothing. What would happen now?

"Don't worry, lassie." Awkwardly the sergeant patted her hand. "I thought you could use that cup of tea now, and a biscuit to go with it. And" — he got to his feet and picked up his notebook — "we won't be needing this any more."

He ripped out the page of notes he had made of Jeannie's confession, crumpled it up and took it over to the stove, then opened the door and flung it in. They both watched it burn.

"Now nobody need be any the wiser. But let me give you a word of advice, lassie. Running away is never a good idea. It can land you in a whole heap of trouble."

Jeannie smiled through her tears, overwhelmed with relief. "I know. And . . . thank you."

Later, she heard her name called as she walked in a daze down the street away from the police station.

"Jeannie! I thought it was you!" Meg Fraser halted the pony trap beside her. "There's good news, I must tell you. Will is being released."

Somehow Jeannie managed to bite back the "I know" that sprang to her lips. She made herself look surprised and pleased, as if she'd only just heard. "Oh, that's good news, ma'am, you must be so pleased. But we all knew he was innocent." She wasn't sure how good her dissembling was — she hated having to put on an act — but Meg was too excited to notice.

"Would you like a lift back to the farm?"

"Oh — no, ma'am, there's no need for that. Beside you'll want to talk to W — Master Will. You'll have so much to say to each other."

Jeannie hurried off, leaving Meg to continue the short distance down the road to the police station. Meg's eyes narrowed. What could Jeannie have been doing in that part of town? And she seemed confused, not her usual self.

But she dismissed the thought. It really didn't matter. The only thing that did matter right now was that Will was in the clear. Maybe in time he would feel able to tell her where he was that night, but she certainly wasn't going to pressure him to do so.

The weather was all that Isobel could have hoped for, given the time of year. Cold, yes, with the threat of a hard frost once darkness fell, but it was dry and clear, perfect for David's first sight of Braehead.

The journey had been easier than she'd thought, thanks to James Falconer's generosity. He'd provided a car with a driver and a nurse to keep an eye on her and David, and the journey had progressed by easy stages up through England and into Scotland. While Isobel had had to contain her impatience to be home, she had to admit that this way it had been best for David.

But now they were only a few miles from their destination, and she felt the excitement build as she pointed out familiar landmarks to David.

"Once we get round this bend you'll be able to see the farm up on the hill — look, there it is!"

David followed the line of her pointing finger. "Just how I imagined it; you described it so well. There must be a great view from those front windows."

"Yes, and you'll have one of them, I think. They were going to give you the downstairs bedroom at the front. Oh, I can't wait for you to meet my mother." She paused, wondering, not for the first time, how Meg would react to David, remembering the attachment there had once been between Meg and David's father. Meg hadn't seen David since he was a motherless baby; how would she feel about accepting him into her home as her future son-in-law?

She was soon to find out. The car drew up in the farmyard, and there was Meg, with Will, ready to welcome them. As soon as the car stopped Isobel jumped out and ran to her mother.

"Oh, how wonderful to see you again! I've been wishing the miles away. And Will, how you've grown."

She hugged them both, then led them over to the car, where David was being helped out by the nurse and the driver. A folding wheelchair stood nearby.

Meg bit her lip. Poor David, what a first impression to make! She could see that he resented the chair, but clearly the long journey had tired him out and there was no way he was able to stand on his own two feet. But a spell in the fresh country air, with good food to build him up and Dr Jim on hand to keep an eye — well, she was confident they would soon have him on his feet.

She put out a hand to David. "Welcome to Braehead. We're very pleased to have you with us."

244

"Thank you, Mrs Fraser. It's very good of you to have me. I hope I won't be too much of a burden to you."

"Not at all. We've been looking forward to your visit, haven't we, Will?"

As Meg introduced her son, Isobel looked around her, wondering what David would make of Braehead and her family. As usual Meg's clothes were serviceable rather than fashionable, and her dark hair was pulled back into a severe bun. If only she would make a bit more effort with her appearance! Isobel found herself thinking, then felt guilty. Her mother worked hard, that was why the farm was so successful. Appearance wasn't everything.

Later, at supper, she was pleased to see David eating with a good appetite and asking questions about the farm and the neighbourhood.

"You'll meet a good friend of ours tomorrow," Meg was saying. "Dr Jim Nicol and his wife. Their son Donald is away in the army."

"How long has Dr Nicol been here?" David asked.

"Oh, a good few years. He brought both Isobel and Will into the world. He's a wonderful doctor. He'll be sadly missed when he does eventually decide to call it a day."

As she spoke Meg was conscious of an idea. Dr Jim needed a successor; David was a doctor. Put two and two together, and —

But David had been so badly wounded. Would he ever be capable of running a demanding country practice?

★ ★ ★

As promised Dr and Mrs Nicol arrived the next day. Dr Jim was soon talking shop with David, regaling him with tales about life as a country practitioner, while Meg, Ellen and Isobel chatted together.

"What a fine young man!" Ellen commented, sipping her tea. "You've done well there, Isobel. Why, he reminds me strongly of Jim at that age."

Isobel laughed. "Thank you. But like Dr Jim he resents being ill. He finds it so difficult being pushed around in a wheelchair."

"I know. But that nurse his father engaged seems a sensible woman, and of course Jim will help as much as he can. I'm sure David will be back on his feet before too long, but we mustn't rush things."

"Patience is difficult when you're young," Meg put in wryly.

Ellen threw up her hands in horror. "Listen to you! Anyone would think you were an old lady! Perhaps we should be looking for an eligible bachelor for you, Meg!"

Meg smiled and changed the subject, but Isobel was surprised to see a faint blush on her mother's cheek. She was intrigued. Could there be someone special in her mother's life? Some farmer, perhaps, who would appreciate a hardworking wife. That might be it. She couldn't imagine her practical, down-to-earth mother, with her sacking aprons and sturdy boots, falling prey to romantic notions.

Meanwhile Ellen Nicol was speaking excitedly. "Oh, I nearly forgot, I have some very interesting news for you about Dod Grant's farm. You know the only relatives he had are down in the borders somewhere, and they're not interested in moving up here, so the place was going on the market."

"Was?" Meg commented. "Do you mean they've withdrawn it? Might they be going to rent it out?" Already she was making mental calculations; how much rent could she afford to pay for Overton? It would make a big property to run, but there would be the prospect of a good return.

But Ellen's next words ended her speculation. "No, they've had a cash offer, and I hear they've accepted."

"What? Good heavens, who could it be?" Meg was taken aback. She had spent a few sleepless nights thinking about Dod's farm, and whether the new owners would be sympathetic to the Braehead water running across their land. If they refused, as Dod had, then Braehead would still be under threat.

"I don't know who it is," Ellen admitted. "No one local, that's for sure."

"Oh, well, we'll have to wait and see," Meg said. "Once we know I'll have to speak to them about the water."

She tried to sound unconcerned but inwardly she was quite the opposite. All sorts of options were running through her mind. But this wasn't the time. Wanting to distract herself, she went over to David and Dr Jim. "How are you two medical men getting on?"

"Splendidly!" Dr Jim beamed at her. "In fact, I have engaged this young man as my assistant."

"Really? You work fast, Jim! Tell me more."

"Once he's got his strength back after the journey, he's agreed to do the Tuesday morning surgery for me; it will give me a chance to get out to some of the more distant patients. And the wheelchair's not a problem — access to the house is easy enough, as you know. I think he'll manage splendidly."

"What a good idea!" Meg turned to look at David and was pleased with what she saw. Already he seemed to have lost that introspective air he had had ever since he'd arrived. He looked genuinely enthusiastic.

"I'm sure I can manage it," he said, with just a trace of defensiveness. "After all, I just have to sit there."

"Well, I'm sure there's a bit more to it than that," Meg said. She was going to add "as long as you're sure you're up to it" but she bit her tongue. David desperately wanted to prove himself and get back to work again; she just hoped he wouldn't rush things and start before he was really ready.

CHAPTER
TWENTY-TWO

Meg eyed the pile of wood with satisfaction. "Well done, Alec, that will make a great blaze."

"Aye, that it will if the rain holds off."

"Fingers crossed. It's not every day we get to celebrate an armistice."

"It's been a long time in coming. Too long for some."

"True enough, I'm afraid." Meg sighed. "But Dr Jim and his wife will be pleased — Donald will be home again soon, safe and sound. Now I'll go and see how the food is coming along and I'll ask Will to help you with the last load of wood."

She turned and went indoors. The end of the war: definitely a cause for celebration! She was anxious that the planned festivities should go well, and the kitchen was busy with baking. Isobel and the nurse were helping, and extra hands had been enlisted from the village. There were crates of beer for the farmhands, sherry for the ladies, and even some long-hoarded champagne for the family party to enjoy later.

Meanwhile there was a lot to do. But strangely there was no sign of Ina or Jeannie. Meg frowned. Where had they got to? This was no time for slacking. Could the girls be upstairs?

She went up the narrow stairs that led off the kitchen, knocked at the door of Ina's tiny room and put her head round. The room was empty. Meg shook her head at the sight of the unmade bed and automatically she went over to straighten it. As she did so, something caught her eye. She reached down, and from under the pillow she pulled out an opened envelope with a banknote protruding from it. It was addressed to Mrs Fraser, Braehead Farm. On further inspection Meg realized it was the money from the sale of some pullets.

She sat down on the bed, the envelope in her hand. This explained a good deal. Odd sums had been going missing — supposedly in the post — off and on for a while now. She would have to have a few words with Ina once she caught up with her.

There was no sign of Jeannie. Could she be involved, Meg wondered, remembering the financial problems of the Duncan family. But it was unlikely, she thought. Somehow she couldn't believe it of Jeannie and, besides, it was clear that the two girls did not get on.

She stood up. She didn't like confrontations, but she couldn't let this pass. She'd have to find Ina and demand an explanation. If, as Meg suspected, Ina was unable to give one then she'd have to go.

Once downstairs she went through to the dairy and stopped as she heard voices — angry voices.

The first she recognized as Ina. "I know what happened that night, believe me. I saw Will Fraser come in at nearly six in the morning —"

"So?" That was Jeannie. Meg held her breath. "So what? That doesn't prove anything."

250

"Oh yes it does. Especially when I know —" There was a clatter as if something had been knocked on the floor.

Meg frowned. She didn't like eavesdropping. She was about to go in and confront the two of them when she heard Ina say, "You could make it worth my while not to tell. I know you've got something saved up. Well, Andy and me, we have more need of it than you have. If you want to keep your precious Master Will it would be worth your while handing it over. If Mrs Fraser hears what I have to say, then you'll be out of here."

That was enough for Meg. She pushed open the door and went in as if she'd heard nothing. "Ah, Ina, here you are, I want a word with you. Jeannie, there's plenty to do in the kitchen. Could you get along there, please?"

The interview that followed was not pleasant. At first Ina blustered and tried to deny everything, until Meg faced her with the evidence of the letter under her pillow. Then she burst into tears.

"I didn't want to do it, ma'am, but me and my lad, we're saving to get married, and I'm scared that if we can't manage it soon he'll leave me —"

"But, Ina, that's no excuse for theft."

"I know, ma'am, and I'm sorry, really I am. I'll pay it all back, really I will."

"Does Andy know what you've been doing?"

"No!" Ina looked worried. "Please don't tell him, ma'am."

"He has a right to know what sort of girl he was hoping to marry. And what you've been doing is a criminal offence. By rights I should report this to the police."

Ina burst into noisy sobs. Meg thought hard. She hoped Ina had learned her lesson and there was no need to take things further. She remembered her own mental turmoil when Will had been held on suspicion of murder, and the sheer sense of relief when he'd been released. Suddenly she felt very sorry for Ina and Andy.

"I don't see any necessity to involve the police, Ina, as long as I can be sure this sort of thing won't happen again." At Ina's shamefaced nod, Meg went on. "I have a suggestion for you."

Swiftly she outlined her proposal: a new position for Andy and Ina on a farm some fifty miles to the north. "I know they're looking for a new horseman, and I'm sure they could take on an extra maid as well if I have a word. There's a cottage for a married couple, not much of a place, but it would do for a start. Do you think Andy would be willing to take it — and you?"

Ina's face brightened up. "I'm sure he would. It's just what we hoped for. Our own place! Oh, thank you, ma'am."

"Then you go and talk to him about it. You could move up there as soon as everything's arranged. But mind, Ina, I don't want to hear any bad reports of you. This is your chance to make a fresh start."

"I know, ma'am. And thank you."

Meg watched her hurry off across the yard in search of Andy. She hoped she was doing the right thing and that Ina had learned her lesson. At least now she and Andy were being given the chance to make a clean break; what they did with it was up to them. She put the envelope in her pocket and went to find Isobel and David.

As she passed through the kitchen she found Jeannie waiting for her. The girl was very pale, but her expression was resolute.

"I'm sorry you had to hear about me from Ina, ma'am," she said. "I should have told you myself."

Meg tried to understand, but failed. "I don't know what you mean, Jeannie."

"About me and Will. That night in the cottage —"

Meg gave her a quick appraising look, and as she did so she remembered Ina's words. *I know what happened that night.*

"All right, Jeannie," she said quietly. "Let's sit down, shall we?"

The story took only a few minutes to tell, and Jeannie kept her voice steady throughout, though Meg could guess what it cost her. When she finished there was silence.

Meg broke it at last. "This explains a lot: Will refusing to say where he was the night Dod Grant was killed. You were the person he was trying to protect."

"Yes, ma'am." Jeannie's voice was a mere thread. "But I did go to tell them. That day you met me in Aberdeen, I'd just been to the police station, but then it was all right anyway — they'd found who did it."

"It must have taken a lot of courage to go to them. Not everyone would have believed your story."

"But you do, don't you, ma'am?"

Meg reached out and squeezed the girl's hand. "Yes, I do. And I'm only sorry you were so unhappy that you tried to run away. We must see what we can do about getting you a place at college."

Jeannie stared in disbelief. "You mean, after all I've done, all the trouble I caused, you'd still help me?"

"I think you'll make a first-rate teacher, Miss Duncan. Don't tell me that Will has been getting those good grades for his homework all by himself. No, it's plain where your talents lie, and it's not as a kitchen maid. Nor as a laundry worker for your mother."

Jeannie looked worried. "But she needs help —"

"I know she was counting on your help. But we'll find someone for her, don't you worry about it."

"Oh, thank you, ma'am! I don't know how I'll ever repay you!"

"By getting these clootie dumplings cooked, that's how. Now I must go and find my daughter."

Knowing that Jeannie needed a bit of time to herself, Meg left the kitchen and hurried back to the front parlour. She was thoughtful as she walked along; might there be something between Will and Jeannie after all? But they were both young yet. If there was any sort of attraction it would have to stand the test of time. Meanwhile, there were other things to sort out.

She found Isobel and David in the parlour, sitting by the fire. There was an air of suppressed excitement about them that instantly put all thought of Jeannie out of her head. "What's going on?" she asked. "You're up to something, I know you are!"

Isobel came over and hugged her. "David's got some wonderful news. You'd never guess."

Meg allowed herself to be guided to a seat next to David. "Well, if I'd never guess you'd better tell me then. What is it?"

David grinned. "It's Overton Farm. You know how it's been sold?"

"Dod Grant's place, yes. Are you saying you know who's bought it?"

"Yes. My father."

Meg made an exclamation of surprise, but David hurried on. "He's bought it for us — to live in once we're married. Because we'd like the wedding to be next spring, if you'd be happy with that, Mrs Fraser?"

"Of course I would!" Meg took Isobel's hand in hers. "I'd be delighted. That's wonderful news."

"And I'll walk down the aisle — no more wheelchairs for me," David promised. "Just try and stop me."

Meg had to blink back the tears. She wouldn't be losing her daughter. Isobel would be less than three miles away, just along the road. And David would doubtless be taking more and more of the work from Dr Jim's shoulders; in time he would probably be able to take over the practice. Everything was working out so well.

But at the back of her mind was a little speck of disappointment. She'd begun to wonder if James would buy the farm himself, to be close to David and Isobel. Now it seemed he'd had no such intentions. She'd see him for the wedding certainly, but presumably after that he'd go back and take up his old life in England. Of course. She'd been foolish to think otherwise.

James Falconer was coming to Braehead. Isobel had given Meg the news in a flurry of excitement.

"He wants to take us all out for a meal to celebrate our engagement. And of course he wants to have a look at Overton, see what needs doing."

"Quite a lot, actually," Meg answered. "Dod Grant wasn't much of a one for creature comforts. The kitchen is primitive; I don't know how his housekeeper managed all these years."

She spoke unconcernedly, but inwardly Isobel's announcement had made a big impression. So James was coming to view his son's new home. Then he'd go back south and, for all Meg knew, that might be the last time she'd set eyes on him until the wedding. But maybe that was the best way; she could get on with her life just as before.

"You'll have to get something new to wear," she said to Isobel. "You've lost so much weight, none of your things fit."

Isobel laughed. "I'm doing my best! Eating my porridge every morning! But yes, it would be good to have a new outfit. Is that dressmaker I used to go to still there?"

"Yes, she is. Why not go to see her this afternoon?"

"Will you come? Perhaps you'd like to get something new yourself."

"Me?" Meg was dismissive. "My blue serge suit is perfectly serviceable." She waved away Isobel's protests.

"And anyway I'm far too busy to be gallivanting around town."

But a week later she allowed herself to be persuaded to accompany Isobel to pick up the finished outfit. As it happened she had business in town anyway, and she had to admit to an interest in how Isobel would look for this important occasion. She wanted James to see what a good recovery his future daughter-in-law had made.

"You look lovely, darling." Her heart was full as Isobel stood before her in the newly finished dress. If only her father had been here to see her. He would have been so proud.

Isobel smiled at the dressmaker. "It's just what I wanted. Mrs Mackie has excelled herself. And look at this." She pointed to another dress hanging in a corner of the room. "Isn't this lovely? And what a shame it's a cancellation. All that work for nothing!"

"It is very nice." Meg had already noticed the dress. "I hope you find another customer for it, Mrs Mackie."

"Why don't you try it?" Isobel suggested suddenly. "It looks your size, and even if it isn't quite it could easily be altered in time for the weekend."

"Isobel, I already have a perfectly good outfit —"

But even as she spoke Meg was conscious that for once she was weakening. If this was the last time she would see James for a while, wouldn't it be good to make the effort to dress up? So that his memory of her was not of a woman in an old serge suit but someone who looked . . . well, more feminine? And the dress was

257

lovely, in a soft slate-blue shade of crêpe de Chine, simply styled. Just the sort of thing she might have chosen for herself years ago.

"Well . . ."

A few minutes later she was looking at herself in the cheval mirror, genuinely surprised at the change in her appearance.

"Mother, you look lovely!" There was a catch in Isobel's throat as she spoke. "You must buy it."

"Oh, I don't know." Meg felt uncharacteristically at a loss. The woman looking back at her was not the Meg Fraser she recognized. It was more like an earlier Meg, one she thought had disappeared long ago.

Suddenly her mind was made up. Why not? She would show that she wasn't afraid of James Falconer, that she didn't have to hide behind unflattering clothes, that she could make the effort if she decided to. "All right," she said quickly, before she could change her mind. "I'll take it."

Isobel ran over and hugged her. "I'm so glad." She exchanged a rather guilty look with the dressmaker. "Oh, and I have a confession to make —"

"You don't need to. I know what you're going to say. But how did you get my measurements?"

"Oh, I went through your wardrobe with a tape measure — and Mother, some of those clothes are ancient! You must throw most of them out."

"Just because you've persuaded me to buy one dress don't think you can reorganise my wardrobe!" Meg wagged a finger at her daughter. "I don't need high fashion for working on the farm."

The weekend arrived and with it the prospect of James Falconer's visit. Meg determinedly spent the day occupied with her usual activities. If nothing else it kept her mind off the coming encounter.

Isobel put her head out of the window and called down. "Mother! Isn't it time you came in and got changed? David's father will be here soon. Or are you coming out to dinner in a sacking apron and tackety boots?"

Meg laughed. "It might set a new fashion! No, I just want to see to the horse that was lame; Alec put a poultice on her last night. Then I'll be in to get dolled up. Shouldn't you be getting ready?"

"I'm just waiting for Jeannie Duncan. She said she'd come and give me a hand with my hair. She'd be glad to help you too if you like."

"We'll see."

Meg was unusually silent when she looked over the horse with the foreman, even though the animal seemed to be making a good recovery. Her mind was on the outfit she'd bought; it was the sort of thing she hadn't worn for about twenty years. Quite different from her normal plain clothes. Would it turn out to be a terrible mistake? Would James think she was wearing something much too young for her? Or worse still, trying unsuccessfully to impress him?

Her courage almost failed her when later she brought it out from the wardrobe and held it up in front of her to look in the mirror. She frowned. Well, she didn't have to wear it. Her navy blue serge suit was perfectly serviceable, and anyway this was Isobel's day, not hers; what she wore was immaterial. She was about to put the crêpe de Chine outfit back in the wardrobe when there was a tap on the door and Jeannie put her head round.

"I'm sorry to bother you, Mrs Fraser, but Isobel wondered if you'd like me to help you with your hair. I've just finished doing hers." She came forward, then stopped in amazement. "Oh, Mrs Fraser, oh, that dress —"

"It's not suitable, is it, Jeannie?" Meg threw it down on the bed. "I'd be better with my serge suit."

"Oh no, not at all, the dress is lovely. It's just that it's, well, so unlike what you usually wear."

"Exactly. Now where did I put that suit?"

"Mrs Fraser!" Jeannie's tone surprised Meg. She turned to face her. "I'm sorry if I'm speaking out of turn," the girl went on, "but I really think you should wear this dress. It's not every day you celebrate your daughter's engagement. And the colour suits you so well."

"You really think so? But my hair . . ."

"I can help you with that. Just sit down here, and I'll show you what I can do with your hair. Then maybe you'll feel differently about the dress."

Meg gave up. For once she had to admit she was not in control of the situation. She let Jeannie style her hair into a simple loose knot, and then when Jeannie had gone to see if Isobel needed any more help, she put on the new outfit.

When she looked in the mirror she could scarcely believe her eyes. It seemed like a different person. There was a little cry behind her, and she spun round to find Isobel, staring as if she had seen a ghost.

"Mother, you look wonderful! I can hardly believe it's you!"

Meg felt embarrassed. "Nonsense! And in any case I'll be back to my normal self in the morning." She patted her hair. "I hope these pins don't fall out. I feel much safer with it in a bun. Should I —"

"No!" Isobel answered firmly. "And anyway there's no time. I came to tell you David's father is here, he's waiting downstairs."

"Oh." Meg took a deep breath. It was now or never. "All right then, let's go down."

With Isobel behind her she went down the stairs and into the front parlour where James stood with David. James had his back to her as she entered the room; it was David who saw her first.

"Good heavens — I mean, Mrs Fraser, you look — that is —"

His father turned round. Meg, watching him intently, saw the expression on his face: first sheer surprise, then appreciation, then something else. There was a little silence, then abruptly James stepped forward. His voice was gruff.

"Meg, I don't know what to say. You've gone to so much trouble —"

"It's not every day we celebrate an engagement."

"No."

He looked cast down and, conscious of having said the wrong thing, she hurried on, "And it's not every day we meet an old friend either. Welcome to Braehead, James."

"I'm glad to be here."

He took both her hands in his and kissed her on the cheek. It was a brief contact only, but the effect it had on Meg was electric. She drew back quickly, looking into his eyes, and what she read there made her heartbeat quicken.

All through the meal that followed she was aware of his gaze, but it was only at the end of the evening that they got a little time together. James leaned over to her as they sat at the table finishing off their coffee. "Would you like a little walk outside if it's not too cold? I think these two might like a bit of time to themselves."

Meg smiled. "That's a good idea."

Her pulse was so loud in her ears she could almost swear it must be audible, and as he helped her on with her coat she was very conscious of his light touch on her shoulders. Outside they were met with a glorious sight — arching rainbows of colour soaring into the night sky.

James stared up at it. "Why, that must be the aurora!"

"Yes, the heavenly dancers as they call them up here. It's a very good display, must have been put on for our benefit."

James said nothing for a few moments as they watched the sky together. Then he said quietly, "Meg, I've had a lot of time for thought these past weeks. And seeing you again has made me even more sure. I want to sell up my business and move up here. I'm sick of the rat race down south."

Meg ran her tongue over her suddenly dry lips. "I see. Of course you'll want to be close to David and Isobel."

"Yes. But there's more to it than that." He turned to her and took her hands in his. "When we parted all those years ago, I thought that was the end for us. But I never forgot you, never stopped loving you. Now, incredibly we've been given a second chance. I'd like to take it. Do you feel the same?"

Meg closed her eyes. She thought of Alistair, the times they'd shared. Genuinely happy times. She had loved him dearly, he was a good man. How would he feel about her returning to her first love? Was it a betrayal?

She opened her eyes to see James looking down at her, his face anxious as he awaited her reply. Behind him the aurora flickered in shimmering shades of green and red.

"I'm asking you again, to marry me, Meg," he said quietly. "Not straight away maybe — we must let the youngsters have their day first. I think I decided weeks ago, when you first came down to Kent to see Isobel. All the old feelings came flooding back." He paused a moment, then he went on. "But if you don't feel the same, you only have to say. I'll find myself a place somewhere else and —"

"No, don't do that." Meg smiled up at him. "Yes, I'll marry you, James."

She stepped forward into his embrace, feeling as if she was coming home. Any doubts melted away. The past held happy memories but this was a time for new beginnings.

At last they drew apart. James smiled down at her. "Shall we go and break the news?"

Meg nodded and took his hand. With a last glance at the blazing sky, she walked beside him into their new life together.

Also available in ISIS Large Print:

The Path to the Lake

Susan Sallis

Viv's marriage to David was not a conventional one, but when he died — in an accident for which she blamed herself — it was as if her whole world had collapsed around her. She escaped by running, mainly around the nearby lake, which was once a popular place of recreation but was now desolate and deserted. It became both her refuge and her dread.

But through the misery she made some unexpected friends — a couple in the village whose family needed her as much as she needed them. And gradually, as a new life opened up, she was able confront the terrible secrets that had haunted her and which could now be laid to rest . . .

ISBN 978-0-7531-8466-0 (hb)
ISBN 978-0-7531-8467-7 (pb)

Megan

Carole Llewellyn

It is 1919 and poverty in the mining village Nantgarw, where 16-year-old Megan Williams lives, forces her to leave her loving family to work as a kitchen maid in Bristol. Her sly cousin Lizzie is already a parlour maid at Redcliffe House and is determined to make things difficult for Megan. It was never going to be easy, for both upstairs and downstairs it is a maelstrom of feuds and jealousies. Megan finds herself a pawn in the battle for power between the two sons of the house, the lustful Harold Fothergill and Robert, recently returned shell-shocked from Flanders battlefields.

But Megan finds friends as well as enemies and in the darkest of times she has to call upon all the courage and determination in her character in order to help her distraught family. But has she lost her own chance of happiness in the process?

ISBN 978-0-7531-8398-4 (hb)
ISBN 978-0-7531-8399-1 (pb)

No Sin to Love

Roberta Grieve

Young Dolly Dixon is determined to overcome her illegitimate background and lead a respectable life, attending evening classes in an attempt to better herself. But when her mother runs off with a lover, she is forced to leave her office job to look after her unappreciative stepfamily.

Her life of drudgery is brightened by her love for handsome market trader Tom Marchant. It is not just his good looks and devastating smile that have won her heart. He is ambitious too and longs to escape his youthful involvement with the criminal Rose brothers. Dolly believes him and at the start of World War II they get married and leave London to open a shop in a Sussex village. But have they really seen the last of the brothers? And what is the other secret that Tom is hiding?

ISBN 978-0-7531-8364-9 (hb)
ISBN 978-0-7531-8365-6 (pb)

Muddy Boots and Silk Stockings

Julia Stoneham

It's 1943 and the country is at war. Yet on one remote Devonshire farm the days are not so dark. An unlikely group of land girls are finding out about life, love and loss, forming surprising friendships along the way.

When Alice Todd's husband runs off with another woman, she is forced to find a means to provide for herself and her young son. Accepting a position as a hostel warden at an old Devonshire farmhouse, Alice finds herself looking after a group of ten volunteer land girls.

The job is not as easy as it first seems. Not only does Alice have to deal with the uncompromising farm owner and her resentful and unhelpful assistant Rose, but as her young charges arrive at the farm, she discovers every girl has a story — and some have rather dark secrets.

ISBN 978-0-7531-8186-7 (hb)
ISBN 978-0-7531-8187-4 (pb)